Jack And Di
Rum Song

Many thanks and much love,
not just now but always,
to my family and friends.

And a special thank you
to all my Facebook islanders.
The first book in this little series
grew through you, and
I love joining you on
di island every day.

If you would like to visit
di Facebook island, go to
www.facebook.com/livelikeajimmybuffettsong

"Fifteen men on a dead man's chest, yo-ho-ho and a bottle of rum! -Robert Louis Stevenson, Treasure Island.

Chapter 1

Memories are like fine bottles of rum, stoppered and stored on a rack in the dusky ship's hold of our minds. They age with time, becoming more mellow and sweet, losing many of the sharp, biting characteristics they may have once had. We pull these bottles out to help us through a rough patch in our lives, to share with friends, or to enjoy during a quiet moment of solitude. And the best part is, these bottles never run dry; the rum will never be gone, as long as we remember to remember.

A fine collection of these rums help punctuate our existence; the years tend to blend together after a while if we don't do things that stand out from our normal day to day lives. I think time begins to fly by as we grow older because we fall more and more into routines and spend so many of our waking hours just trying to get through the day. We need those special rum times to slow down and savor our lives or they will feel very short indeed.

The racks in my own hold had been filling up nicely with a fine variety of rums over the last year, although my life hadn't always been so memorable.

There was a time when every day seemed to be the same, a blur of bland days stretching out behind me into my far aft horizon. You see, I used to have a high paying gig at Image Makers, a public relations firm in the Minneapolis area, where I spent my working days polishing corporation's images so they could earn a few more quarterly points. And I had an expensive condo full of Ikea furniture, where I lived with my not so nice, skinny blonde girlfriend Brittany. But one day a Peterbilt truck almost squashed me, I went on a week long bender in a Ramada Inn, and Jimmy Buffett came to me in a pepperoni pizza induced dream and told me to stop being a putz; so I did. I quit the job, lost the girl, sold most of my stuff, and packed the rest into my new old rusty red Cadillac convertible, and hit the road to live my life like a Jimmy Buffett song.

And for the most part I managed to do it, too, although I soon found out that while someone like Jimmy can give you a rhythm to live by, the songs are yours to write. It's like you're one of the many trop rockers paying their dues along the coasts, always adding new songs to the fabric of the beach bum lifestyle. I may have wasted away a time or two too, but when I did, I did it my way, which was always slightly different from Jimmy's.

My name is Jack Danielson, and I love filling those rum bottles with memories and living my songs.

I'd spent the last year of my life since my escape from the ordinary living in a small room above a store just off Duval Street in Key West, Florida. A day in my life often began with breakfast with the roosters over at the Blue Heaven, followed by an hour or two nap on the beach. By then it would be time for what disguised itself as work, bartending in an open air establishment, which was really a chance to meet people from all over the world and listen to whatever band was playing that afternoon, and get paid for doing both. Sometimes I'd go down to Mallory Dock for the sunset celebration and sell a couple of the paintings I'd been getting better and better at creating, and have some of Mike's conch fritters and his key lime iced tea, then watch for the green flash at sunset. And those were the average days.

It was a pretty damned fine life and I hadn't been looking to change it, other than to find a new girl to replace Haley, my brunette honeysuckle who'd moved back to Denver for some reason I couldn't fathom such as missing winter. Me, I was quite prepared to continue on my present course towards eternal contentedness if it killed me; it would have been a great way to go.

At least that was the plan until I got the letter.

It was from an attorney, usually not a good thing, and it concerned my uncle, which seemed odd at the time since I didn't even know I had one. Some guy named Billy Danielson, who had passed away and evidently left me something in his will. I called my parents to ask about him, and the first comment out of my father's lips was *"Oh, hell,"* followed by a lot of silence on the line.

"Hello?" I said finally. "Are you still there?"

"Yes, I'm still here," said my father.

"Are you alright? Who was this guy anyway?" I said.

My father was silent again for a moment, then said, "He was my brother."

"Wow. I'm sorry, Dad," I said.

"It's alright; just a bit of a surprise. We haven't seen each other or spoken in years," said my father.

"What happened, anyway? Why don't I know him?" I said.

"It's a long story," said my father. "Back in nineteen sixty-nine when they started the draft Billy and I got called up, and we both went; me to Vietnam, and Billy to Canada. Your grandfather was furious; you know how he was. His own father had died in World War Two, and he felt Billy had dishonored his memory and the family. So he disowned him, and told him never to come back, and made me swear never to speak about him again."

"Grandpa was such a bastard; I never liked him," I said.

"Well, he was my father, and we honored his wishes. I'm not proud of it, though," said my father. "I did hear from Billy occasionally, but finally I lost all track of him about twenty years ago; the last I heard he was in the Caribbean somewhere. You know, he's your godfather, too. Your mom did that; really ticked off your grandfather, but she hated the whole thing."

"Why didn't somebody tell me about him after Grandpa died?" I asked.

"It seemed pointless, for one thing," said my father. "I never thought we'd hear anything from him again. *And* I didn't want you running off to find him; Billy was a bit of a nut case, and a hippie, and I was afraid it might run in the family; your mother's uncle was the same way, and he wandered to Africa and got eaten by hyenas. Looking at your life now I see I was right to worry."

We talked for a few more moments, mostly about where my life was currently headed, now that my father had managed to bring it up in the conversation. Then we said our goodbyes and hung up.

With all this new information in hand I seriously thought about just throwing the letter away and ignoring the whole thing. But the letterhead showed it had come from a tropical island, and with my Buffett song pledge there was no way I could pass up on an excuse to visit it.

It would be wrong in more ways than I could count, and at the very least it might make for a good bar story.

So I called the number on the letter and got an annoying buzzing sound on the other end of the line for my trouble. I tried again that evening and got the same thing, as well as all the next day. On the third day I finally got irritated enough to actually read the letter thoroughly, and found that I'd missed the part where it said I'd have to show up in person to collect my inheritance; which was what I wanted to do anyway. So I gave up on trying to get through on the phone and concentrated on figuring out how to get there instead.

I didn't exactly remember seeing any specials about di island on the Travel Channel, or any pop ups popping up on my laptop beckoning me whenever I booked a hotel on Expedia. When I checked I found that Wikepedia was just as much in the dark as I was, but just before exhausting my Googling skills I finally discovered a few of meager bits of information about the place. First, it did exist. Second, it was a small island, about two miles across in either direction, situated southward of the British Virgin Islands. Other than that, the only things I could figure out was that their major exports were sugar cane and goat's milk, and that it seemed damn near impossible to get to.

But I happened to be friends with someone that knew the waters of the Caribbean like the back of his hand (or so he claimed), and often even more intimately from falling off his boat into them. We'd stayed in touch since my first voyage and fishing trip aboard the Lazy Lizard, and had sailed together many a time since and drank many a Chesterita.

I rang his number, hoping he hadn't recently fallen into the ocean with his cell phone again.

"Crazy Chester's Bar and Boat Stop, this is Crazy Chester, and yes I am, so don't ask."

"Chester! It's Jack," I said.

"Sparrow?" said Chester.

"Danielson," I said.

"Dang it; still waiting," said Chester.

Crazy Chester ran a nice little eclectic ship wreck of a bar in the middle Keys, and owned a small charter fishing boat he'd christened "The Lazy Lizard". He was a nice little guy, a bit quirky perhaps, maybe even insane, but then all the best people were. His biggest claim to fame was that he hadn't worn a shirt or shoes for going on eight years now, and had no intention of ever doing so again.

I told him where I was trying to get to, and asked if he'd heard of the place.

"Heard of it? I go there all the time!" said Chester. "But why do you need to go?"

"It's a long story," I said.

"Then never mind; I've got mahi-mahi on the grill," said Chester.

"Any chance you could take me there?" I asked.

"Hm. I'm not sure when. The Lizard is out of commission at the moment," he said.

"What did you do to it this time?" I asked.

"I ran over a reef," said Chester. "But I almost got that damned seagull this time."

Chester's arch nemeses were seagulls. "I still don't believe anyone can tell them apart," I said.

"*I* can," said Chester. "I could take you sooner or later, but if you're in a hurry why don't you just go to Jost Van Dyke and sit in the Soggy Dollar?"

I didn't see how sitting in wet currency was going to help me get to di island, but it wouldn't have been the first time Chester had said something crazy. "Soggy dollar?" I said.

"It's a bar in the British Virgin Islands; you'll like it," said Chester. "Just sit there until Gus Grizwood shows up; he's a seaplane pilot that stops into my bar here from time to time, but he loves the Soggy Dollar. He'll take you to di island."

"And if he doesn't show up?" I said.

"He will. He can't go more than three days without a Painkiller. I'll pop in for a visit on di island when I get the Lizard running again; gotta go," said Chester, and he hung up.

That settled that. Chester had a way of saying things that made it seem like I'd already made up my mind, so by the time I was off the phone I was already thinking about the Virgin Islands and how to get to them.

So three days later, my few belongings packed and my current but very replaceable Key West job lost, I stepped off a plane onto Beef Island Airport on the isle of Tortola in the British Virgin Islands. I was ready to begin my quest for Gus and transportation to di island. And after a few days of searching by way of sitting in the Soggy Dollar Bar drinking Painkillers, I tracked down my prey.

"Rum is made using sugarcane by-products like molasses or sugarcane juice, by fermentation and distillation."

Chapter 2

Gus Grizwood was a seaplane pilot, tanned and grizzled as his name suggested, who'd switched from a life flying air taxis for Delta to island hopping tourists all around the Caribbean. He said he flew an old Noorduyn Norseman aircraft, to which I responded by nodding knowingly of course, even though I had no idea what the hell he was actually talking about; until he took a picture out of his wallet and showed me, that is.

It was a lovely little yellow plane, with nice rounded lines like an old Studebaker. It was built in the late thirties, back when, Gus said, they still had an effing clue what things should look like. Upon seeing her photo I instantly wanted a ride in her, and hopefully to di island, but when I broached the subject to Gus the conversation turned into something like this...

"You want to go where? Ha, ha, ha, hee, ha, har haw," and so on.

After Gus had settled down a bit and stopped spitting all over the place, I tried again.

"I'm serious. I really need to get to di island," I said earnestly.

"Look, nobody ever *needs* to get to di island," said Gus. "It's just not that kind of place."

"Well, I do," I said. "I have business there."

I waited for Gus to stop laughing again, then explained to him about the letter, Billy, and my inheritance.

A serious look came over his face, then he pushed up his cap a bit and scratched his head, and said, "Fine, it's your dollar. I doubt if there's anything on the whole effing island that's worth what you've already paid to get down here and are going to have to pay me to take you the rest of the way, but if you really want to go..."

"So you will take me then?" I asked.

"Yeah, it's what I do; charge idiots like you big wads of money to fly them wherever their little hearts desire," said Gus. "When do you want to leave?"

I wasn't sure I liked being called an idiot, but then again since I was stupid enough to consider putting my life in the hands of a guy slamming Painkiller after Painkiller, it was hard to argue with him about my IQ. "How about tomorrow morning?" I said.

"Works for me," said Gus. "Eleven fifty-nine in the harbor then?"

"Er, why eleven fifty-nine?" I said.

"Because that's the earliest I fly in the AM," said Gus, hoisting another Painkiller in the air.

"Fine," I said. "I don't want to screw up your schedule."

"Smart man. You wouldn't want to see me in the morning; you wouldn't like me in the morning," said Gus. "And I definitely wouldn't like you."

The next morning (but just barely) I met Gus down at the harbor. I easily spotted his brightly colored plane amongst all the boats, and found him already doing his pre-flight checks, having turned, like any good aviator, into the consummate pilot when it counted. He was in far better shape than I would have expected, a sure sign of an alcohol seasoned pro, for which I was thankful; if you were gonna drink as heavily as Gus appeared to, you better know how to recover from it when your work took place thousands of feet off the ground.

We said our hellos, and after handing him the big wad of cash that we idiots paid as our fee, he motioned me on board. Moments later the engine roared to life, and one of those rum memories I'll treasure forever began.

It's hard to describe the exhilaration of going from the sea into the air; most of us don't spend enough time in either, keeping our feet firmly planted on terra firma for the bulk of our lives. We taxied slowly out into open water, then Gus opened up the throttle and we began zipping along, turquoise agua speeding by faster and faster as it sparkled in the bright afternoon (but just barely) sun. Soon the choppiness of the water disappeared and the ride smoothed, and I realized we were suddenly airborne.

As Gus steered a course towards di island, I looked out my window at a view that was nothing short of spectacular. I've only been in the air a few times but I can't imagine there are many places more beautiful to look down upon than the islands of the Caribbean. Unfortunately it wasn't a particularly long flight, about an hour, although Captain Grizwood took his time and circled some of the other islands to at least try and give me some of my money's worth. But it was unforgettable, helped along by the fact I was flying in a classy vintage plane. Too soon we landed back in the ocean, another wonderful experience, and began taxiing in towards my destination.

It occurred to me that I hadn't seen di island from above; Gus had neglected to circle that. When I asked him about it as we came to a stop at one of the old docks in the tiny harbor, he chuckled and said he figured I'd want to experience it for the first time from eye level. What he meant by that I didn't know and didn't find out. He quickly got my bags out of the back of the plane, gave me his card, and said, "Good luck; when you're ready to leave give me a call and I'll be here in a

17

day or two." Then he tipped his hat, cast off his lines, taxied back out and flew away, dipping his wings a couple of times in goodbye as he went.

I stood there with the dock swaying and creaking beneath me and surveyed my surroundings. The harbor was home at the moment to a handful of vessels, from a couple of old commercial fishing boats to a half submerged skiff that reminded me of Captain Jack's arrival in Port Royal. On the shore sat a row of mismatched wooden and concrete buildings; only two were marked, with signs that read *"Bate and Takkle Shop"* and *"Da Fish Gutter"* respectively. The scene looked like a low budget set from Jaws 17.

I suddenly felt very much alone and very far from home, both of which were quite accurate. I hadn't really thought the whole thing through, and it now seemed like being on an unknown, secluded, and very foreign island all by myself without a clue what I was in for wasn't perhaps the best of situations. This was the sort of occasion where the gringo from the states ended up being kidnapped and ransomed for his bartending fortune, or hacked into tiny pieces with a rusty machete and sent home in a dozen small boxes. Or both.

Of course no one actually had to kidnap me; all they really had to do was take my cell phone away and I'd be pretty much screwed, stuck on di island until I agreed to their demands, which would probably at the very least involve my participation in some ancient and indecent island ritual involving a goat. Then again, there was no one in sight, so it was equally possible the entire population had been eaten by same said goats, who had by now turned carnivorous in retribution for the rituals.

While my imagination went wandering off by itself, my eyes spied a small building at the end of the dock marked *"Customs."* I decided to get whatever was going to happen to me over with before my overactive mind turned all di islanders into singing zombies belting out off-key renditions of *"Kokomo"* while they chased me around di island.

So I picked up my bags and made my way down the unsteady dock, which was a lot like walking on one of those rope bridges that Indiana Jones types favored. I made it to the end and stepped off, happy to find that di island itself at least seemed steady enough, then walked up to the red wooden door in the side of the building and knocked.

There was no answer, and no sounds came from within. I tried again and got the same response, and worried momentarily that perhaps the goats had already been there, too. Then I tried the knob and found it unlocked, and opened the door and stepped inside.

I found a tiny office, very neat, almost out of place with what I'd seen outside. A few pictures of fish, flowers, and ferns hung on the walls, as well as a mounted goat's head (one at least had lost the food chain battle). A dark man in a red suit jacket sat leaning way back in a chair, his feet up on his desk, fast asleep.

I wasn't sure what to do at first, since I didn't want to just stand there clearing my throat until he woke up; it seemed rude somehow. But then I noticed a bell sitting on the desk with a sign that read *"Ring for service"*, so I did. For some reason dinging the annoying but familiar metal thing seemed perfectly acceptable to me.

The man stirred slowly; I would have jumped clear out of my skin, but he awoke as if to the sound of three little birds pitched by his doorstep singing sweet songs, as opposed to the clanging of Big Ben. He opened his eyes and looked at me, then blinked them a couple of times and cocked his head to one side, as if in mild surprise.

"Can I help you, mon?" he said finally.

"Yes, I need to check in," I said stupidly, carrying on with my silver bell ringing behavior. "To di island!" I added quickly, in the hope it would make me seem less stupid.

I could tell by the look on his face that it didn't work. He took his feet off the desk and sat up in his chair, then motioned for me to sit down. I dropped my bags on the floor and sat in one of the wooden chairs facing his desk.

"Passport please," he said.

I took it out of one of my cargo pockets and handed it to him. He opened it and looked it over, then me. "Are you carrying any fruit, vegetables, or live animals?" he asked.

"No," I said. I found I felt safer already; funny how some good old-fashioned bureaucracy made me feel at home.

"And what is di nature of your visit to di island?" he asked.

I took the letter about the will out and gave it to him, and he examined it with a blank expression on his face and handed it back to me. "And how long will you be staying on di island?" he asked.

I thought about it. "I don't really know," I said finally. "Is there a time limit?"

He looked at me again, then said, "No. But no visitor stays on di island for very long."

"I see," I said. I sat staring at him and he sat staring at me; I couldn't tell if we were finished with my temporary immigration or not. "Is that it? Can I go now?"

He slid my passport back to me across the desk and said, "Yes. You may go now to di island."

"Thank you," I said, and stood up.

"Unless you wish to talk to di island attorney about your inheritance," he said.

"The attorney is here?" I asked, sitting back down.

The man nodded, then stood up and walked slowly across the room to the far corner and took off his red suit jacket and hung it on a peg. Then he took down a blue pinstriped one and carefully put it on and brushed it off, and walked back behind his desk and sat down. Finally he reached out and turned the brass sign on his desk around so that it no longer read *"Gerald Wonbago: Customs Officer"*, and instead said, *"Gerald Wonbago: Attorney At Law."*

"May I see di letter please?" said Mr. Wonbago.

I got it out again and handed it to him, and he looked it over slowly. "And your passport please," he said.

"But you just saw my passport a minute ago," I said, somewhat irritably.

"Dat was di custom's officer," Wonbago said matter-of-factly, with the same expression on his face as all the evil ladies down at the DMV.

I sighed and dug out my passport again, and handed it to him.

He examined both of my documents for some time, then said, "Everyting seems to be in order," then took a form out of a drawer in his desk and filled in some blanks upon it. Then he slid it and a pen across the desk towards me and indicated a line on it with his finger. "Sign here."

I picked it up and quickly read it over, but didn't see any indication of what it was for; it appeared to be just a vague general statement about the transfer of some goods. "Wait a minute," I said. "How am I supposed to know if I should sign this when I can't tell what I'm agreeing to?"

"Look, mon; we only have di one form for di transfer of all goods and property on di island. It's very simple; you sign di papers and what Billy Danielson left you becomes yours," said Wonbago.

"But what is it he left me?" I asked.

"Di will states that I'm not supposed to tell you dat until after it belongs to you. It says it would spoil di surprise," said Wonbago.

"It's going to spoil it even more when I get back on the plane and fly out of here," I said.

Mr. Wonbago looked out the window behind me that faced the docks. "And what plane be dat, mon?" he asked.

"You've got a point," I said. I'd come this far, anyway; it seemed stupid to turn back now. If I ended up with something I really didn't want, such as a pile of Billy's debt, I seriously doubted if this generic paper I was signing would hold up in any courts.

So I grabbed the pen and quickly signed before I could change my mind, and Mr. Wonbago took it from me and tore off a carbon copy and gave it to me. "Congratulations; come with me," he said, and he stood up and walked out the door, so I grabbed my bags and quickly followed.

When Wonbago got outside he stopped and put his hand up to shade his eyes and scanned the horizon, then whistled, with a decibel level that any taxi hailing New Yorker would kill for. Moments later a lanky, dark skinned, shirtless young man came running up, dreadlocks bouncing as he went.

Wonbago took a set of keys out of his pocket and tossed them to the kid. "Cavin will bring you to your inheritance," he said to me, then said to Cavin, "Dis be Billy's nephew; take him to you know where."

"You mean, you're still not going to tell me what I've inherited?" I said.

"No, mon" said Wonbago. "Your Uncle's will clearly states-"

"Yeah, yeah," I said with a sigh. Cavin was already heading up the slight hill towards the buildings, and I followed. "This had better be good; the suspense is killing me."

"Mount Gay on the island of Barbados appears to be the oldest rum factory in the world, with written proof of distillation in 1703."

Chapter 3

When I caught up to Cavin he had just gone around behind the row of buildings. There was an old topless jeep parked there, green and rusted rust colored, and he climbed inside. "Throw your stuff in the back," he said, and I did, then got in beside him. It took him a few tries to get the vehicle started, but eventually it kicked in with a cloud of smoke and a couple of backfires, and he ground it into gear, and off we rolled.

Cavin turned onto a road of sorts, about as smooth as an Illinois highway, and we bounced along it into the interior of di island. There wasn't a lot to see by any tourist standards, although if you were looking to get away from it all it appeared that di island might be just the place for you. We passed small houses, huts, and farms, and I began to see a few people and a lot of wandering livestock (including some goats who tried to look innocent). Di islanders themselves appeared to be a mixed bunch from all over the hemisphere, and most waved or shouted a friendly greeting to Cavin, and stared at me as we drove past.

While there may not have been any particular places we passed that were worthy of a travel brochure aimed at luring German cruise line passengers, di island itself was quite lovely in its own rugged way. There were plenty of swaying, coconut laden palm trees to go around, along with a fine selection of landscaping ferns, grasses, and brightly colored flowers; I even thought I saw a parrot or some such vivid bird flying through the trees on a couple of occasions. All in all, di island was your standard issue tropical island, and therefore, mostly beautiful.

Even though we'd passed a few people on our short drive, di island population still seemed very tiny to me; I hadn't exactly expected Tokyo, but I thought there might be more than the six humans I'd seen so far, and I asked Cavin about it.

"A lot of people are at work in Rodrigo's sugar cane fields right now," he said. "And many of the one's who aren't are probably either at the bar or fishing; they love to fish on di island."

"You have a bar here?" I asked.

Cavin laughed. "Of course we have a bar; we're not a bunch of cavemen, dude."

"Sorry," I said, chagrined. I should have known better; everyone needed a bar; even said cavemen probably had one. The cavemen might not have had alcohol yet and most likely had to bang their heads with a rock to numb themselves, but at least they weren't sitting at home banging their heads with rocks alone; it was much better to be a social head banger.

"You know, we don't get many visitors around here; you're from the US, right?" said Cavin.

"Yes," I said. "Minnesota. Well, Florida, now."

"Never been to either," said Cavin.

I wasn't too surprised, although the kid did speak very good English. "No?"

"No. I grew up in Cali myself," said Cavin.

"California?" I said, now too surprised.

"Yeah, dude. I got a job working on a cruise ship as a waiter when I got out of high school; I hated it, so I jumped ship in Jamaica," he said. "They were going to kick me out so I hitched a ride with Gus Grizwood and ended up here."

"You know Gus, too?" I asked, still too surprised.

"Everyone knows Gus," said Cavin. "He stops in here every other week or so."

"He failed to mention that when we were negotiating the hefty price tag for my flight," I said evenly.

"I bet he told you how far out of his way this was," said Cavin.

"Something like that," I said.

"Don't feel too bad; Gus is a sneaky bastard," said Cavin. "He gets the best of most people." he pulled the jeep to a sudden stop and turned off the key. "Well, we're here."

I peered up from the floor where I'd been contemplating my revenge on Gus, and looked around. We were parked next to a low stone wall that surrounded a very large, old, dilapidated appearing building. "We're where?" I said.

"At your inheritance," said Cavin, jumping out of the jeep.

I searched three hundred and sixty degrees around me, and found that my bequest was either a rock, a tree, a mule, or the beat up building. After examining the building for a moment I hoped for the mule, but had a sinking feeling.

"This is it?" I said, getting out of the jeep and walking towards the building. "This place? Or can you not tell me yet or it will spoil the surprise?"

Cavin laughed. "No, this is what Billy left you, dude."

I walked halfway down the weed encroached stone path that led to the arched two door entrance, and stopped to get a better look. The structure appeared to be sound, at least from here on the outside, but for all I knew the other three walls had already fallen down. It was definitely a mess and in heavy need of repair, though; most of the faded red shutters that were supposed to cover the windows were either laying on the ground or were about to be. The paint-peeled walls were covered with some kind of a vine that perhaps used to be green but now looked like brambles. And speaking of brambles, my yard was filled with them, and a platoon of scurrying lizards. "No abandoned vehicles to complete my trailer park trash look?" I said.

"They're around the back," said Cavin.

"Ah," I said. The biggest upside I could find was that the property was situated near the ocean, with a stone patio on the left overlooking the sea. "At least it has a nice view. What direction is that?" I asked, pointing.

"West," said Cavin.

So Billy was either smarter than I assumed, or lucky. I figured there should be some nice sunsets from the patio, situated as the building was on a slight hill leading down to the ocean. "Well, let's check out the inside," I said. "If you think it's safe."

"It hasn't fallen down yet," said Cavin.

"That's comforting," I said. We walked to the front doors and I turned the handle on one and pushed inward. It creaked angrily at me but didn't fall off its hinges, and we stepped inside.

If I had thought the outside was a mess I didn't know what one was, really. Light streamed in through the half shuttered windows and several holes in the roof, illuminating an interior filled with pallets, crates, plants, empty barrels and casks, bottles and cans, and light fixtures that had fallen from the ceiling. Pigeons scattered as we walked through the debris, although their droppings that covered everything unfortunately didn't.

It appeared to be an old factory. There were a few big round tanks, as well as two very large metal kettles of some kind that sat on the cement floor of the factory, and I made my way over towards the latter.

"What are these for?" I asked, rapping my knuckles on one. "Chemicals?"

"You could say that," said Cavin.

"I did say that, but was I right?" I said.

"Depends on how you look at it," said Cavin.

"Meaning..." I said. One thing about di islanders; they loved being cryptic.

"They're pot stills. For rum," said Cavin.

"Rum?" I said, surprised.

"Yes, rum," said Cavin. "This is a rum distillery, or was supposed to be."

"Supposed to be?" I asked.

"Billy never got it up and running; he ran out of money," said Cavin.

I stood in the middle of all the mess and tried to process all this information. "So you're telling me," I said slowly, "that my uncle Billy who I never met and didn't even know existed until a few days ago left me a Caribbean rum factory?"

"That's about it, dude," said Cavin.

I'd been right about one thing at least; I definitely had a good story to tell now. At this very moment I could sit in bars and tell people I owned a rum factory in the Caribbean; beat the hell out of saying I was a bartender, no matter how noble it sounded.

"Do these things work?" I said, looking one of the copper stills over. It appeared to be sound, although covered in grime.

Cavin shrugged. "Beats me. They've never been used and are brand new, or at least were when Billy had them brought here years ago. I know that much from the stories."

"The stories?" I asked.

"All the old men sit around and talk about the rum days when Billy was trying to put the whole thing together. Everyone was all excited about actually having a way to make a living besides cutting sugar cane, fishing, and raising goats. But like I said, he never managed to get it open," said Cavin.

"That's a shame," I said.

"Yeah," said Cavin. "So are you gonna do it?"

"Do what?" I said.

"Finish opening the factory," said Cavin.

I looked at him in surprise. "Me? I don't know the first thing about rum, other than I like it too much. And this place is a disaster. No, I was just asking about the stills because I think they're probably worth some money if they're useable."

"You could fix it up," suggested Cavin, looking around him at the factory.

"Yeah, anything is possible, but that doesn't mean I'm going to do it. I'm a big supporter of the avoid work movement these days," I said.

Cavin appeared to be thinking, as if he were trying to find another angle from which to try to persuade me.

"Look," I said. "I'm sure everyone on di island would like me to restart the rum days again, but it's not going to happen. I've got a great, simple life carved out in the Keys, and I'm not going to mess around with some condemned rum factory, no matter how cool it sounds, so forget it."

Cavin shrugged again, then said "It's up to you, dude. But I'd be careful who you say that to; some of the people around here have some pretty strong feelings about the factory."

"My lips are sealed," I said. "I'll stay for a while, check out di island, and make some calls and see what I can find out about these pot stills. Is there some place I can get a room?"

Cavin pointed at the corner to the left of the entrance, where what looked to be an inner office sat. "Billy just slept in there."

"Really?" I said, and walked over to the door of the room and opened it. It was a little cleaner inside, but just barely, seemingly protected from the elements and animals better, as the ceiling was still sound. A desk and chair sat under a window, a small bed resided on one side of the room, and a beat up sofa on the other. Old framed photos hung on the walls, and a potpourri of knickknacks covered some shelves. I went over and patted the mattress on the bed and a cloud of dust flew into the air.

"No, thank you," I said, once I'd finished coughing. "Is there any place else on di island? A hotel or something?"

"Yeah, there's the Coconut Motel," said Cavin. "They always have rooms. But you'll need to go to Monkey Drool's to get a key."

"Monkey Drool's?" I asked. "What or who the hell is that?"

"The bar," said Cavin. "The Innkeeper owns both that and the motel. I can take you there; it's on the other side of di island by the water."

"Lead the way," I said, motioning my guide out the door.

The trip so far hadn't been a total loss, at least; it was interesting, and like I said, a damned fine story. And if I could find someone to buy the pot stills I might even pay for the whole thing. I figured I'd spend a few days hanging around di island, maybe get some sun on the beach, and see if the fishing was as good as everyone seemed to think it was. And now we were heading towards a bar on a nice, hot, tropical day.

It was enough to make a monkey drool.

"Bring me one noggin of rum, now, won't you, matey."

Chapter 4

Cavin dropped me off at the bar, saying he had to return Wonbago's jeep, and I lugged my bags towards the building and in through the saloon style swinging doors. It was dark inside, the only light being that which shone through the doorway, but it was enough to see by. There was a small bar on the opposite wall from the door, and mismatched tables and chairs were scattered around the room. It looked for the most part like any other run down island hangout.

"This bar be closed, matey," said a low, deep, rumbling voice from one of the dark corners.

I jumped, startled, and peered at the corner from where the voice had come, but could only barely make out a figure in the low light my eyes hadn't totally adjusted to, after being in the bright Caribbean sunshine. "I'm sorry," I said. "Cavin dropped me off and said-"

"This bar be closed, matey," said the voice again.

I stood for a moment, not sure what to do, but then the eerie voice spoke again.

"Steer your course to the aft side if it be grog ye be seekin'," it said helpfully, but creepily.

"T-thanks," I stammered. I made my way to the door and pushed it open, and as a shaft of sunlight leapt into the room, turned and glanced quickly back at the corner, where in the dim light I could have sworn I saw...a pirate.

I went outside and shook off my jitters, then walked around to the back and found another bar, this one outside and fully open to the air. It looked like the spot where all di island action probably took place, if there was such a thing. A roof came out from the building covering a large area of sand that passed for a floor. The bar bar itself had been built by putting boards on top of two halves of a longboat that was split down the middle, with the aft end of each butted up against the wall of the building, leaving a space for the bartender in between. A fair number of tables and chairs sat from up by the bar area to all the way out under the sun by the beach.

All sorts of odd decorations adorned the walls, posts, and ceiling. Fishing nets, faded photographs, conch shells, starfish, colored bottles, broken tiles, etc, covered everything, while Christmas lights zigzagged back and forth beneath the beams. But the real centerpiece was a large, badly stuffed monkey of some kind leaning against one of the support posts, holding a coconut mug and sporting a sombrero and an eye patch. He didn't look all that happy for which I couldn't blame him, being dead and stuffed and all that.

Island music played from a boombox on a shelf, completing the scene; that and about a dozen or so of di islanders who sat staring at me in silence.

"Hellooo," I said in my best friendly tone.

A steel drum rendition of *"Tiny Bubbles"* emanating from the boombox was the only reply I got in return, until a short, Latin looking fellow finally raised his hand and said "Hello?" almost as if he were asking me a question.

"Hey, mon," said the bartender. "Do you be Billy's nephew?"

"Well, yes, I am," I said.

"Hey! Hey, everybody! Dis be Billy's nephew from di states!" said the bartender excitedly. "He be di new owner of di rum factory!"

And with that introduction I was met with a flood of greetings, handshakes, introductions, and slaps on the back; I doubt if Jimmy Buffett would have received a warmer island welcome. Once everyone had finished loving me half to death, the bartender proudly said, "I be di Innkeeper, and dis be my place, and you be welcome here. Wat'cho be drinkin'?"

I was feeling pretty good and comfortable now, almost like a celebrity. "Two questions," I said. "Is the beer cold, and do you take American dollars?" I didn't want to run up a bar tab I couldn't pay that was going to get my ass kicked, Caribbean style.

The small Latin gentleman who'd introduced himself as Ernesto said, pointing, "Do you see the light on the wall?"

I looked; it was an old, lit up, Hamm's beer sign, complete with the bear. What it was doing all the way down here in the Caribbean I didn't know. "Yes, I see it," I said.

"When that light is on, that means the power plant is working today, senor," said Ernesto. "And that means the beer is cold."

"Ah. Good signal," I said. "And the dollars?"

"Dollars be good," said the Innkeeper. "Not as good as dey used to be, but we still take dem. But your money be no good today; everyting be on di house."

"That's mighty nice of you," I said, sitting down on a bar stool. I kicked off my flip-flops and stuck my toes in the sand, which felt damned fine as usual. "I'll take whatever beer you carry."

"We have Red Stripe, Kalik and Corona when we can get dem," said the Innkeeper. "Today we have Red Stripe."

"A Red Stripe would be great," I said.

The Innkeeper grabbed me a bottle out of a cooler, opened it, and put it in front of me as the rest of the Monkey Drool's crowd sat down around me. I picked up the stubby, frosty brown bottle and took a drink, and it went down like an old friend, which it was.

"So, you've been to see the factory?" asked a man.

"Yes, I have," I said.

"What did you tink?" said the Innkeeper.

I didn't want to offend any of my new compadres and said, "Very nice. Looks like it was quite the place back in the day."

"So how long?" asked Ernesto.

I took another drink from my beer and was about to ask Ernesto what he meant when I was distracted by a beautiful, brown, suntanned woman who came around the corner and sashayed across the sand (surely not something easy to do), before sitting down on a stool and leaning way back against a post. She had long, raven black hair and seemingly darker eyes, and wore a tiny pair of cutoff jean shorts and a white button down shirt tied above her flat stomach. She reminded me of my beloved Maria, the hula girl who had accompanied me on my dashboard during my odyssey south from Minnesota to the Keys, and even now lay carefully wrapped in my nearby luggage. This human counterpart would have been attractive in almost any setting; here by the ocean on a tropical island in a beach bar she was pretty damned devastating.

She sat staring right at me, which intimidated the hell out of me, of course. There was something about her eyes that seemed different from the women I'd known, almost hypnotic, and I couldn't bring myself to stop gazing back at her in spite of my well honed instinct to be a wuss and look away.

"How long, senor?" I heard Ernesto say again, somewhere in the back of my senses.

"How long for what?" my mouth managed to say, although it was on autopilot while my brain concentrated on the woman.

"How long to open the rum factory?" said Ernesto.

"Oh, that," I said, nonchalantly and almost dreamily. "I don't think I'm going to do that."

"You're not?" asked someone.

"No. I've got this great song going in Key West," I said. "I don't want it to end. I'm just going to see if I can find someone to buy the stills. You folks can have the building though, if you like."

I sat staring back at my Latin island lady, lost in my own world. It was amazingly quiet in it at the moment; too quiet, actually. In fact dead silent, I realized. No one was talking, and even the music had stopped. I finally shook my head a little and looked to see where the tunes had gone, and saw the Innkeeper standing with the unplugged cord of the boombox in his hand and a grim look on his face. "Dat be two dollars for di beer," he said evenly.

I suddenly realized what I'd just done; spilled di beans about my no go plans for di rum factory all over di place, in spite of Cavin's warning. And he'd been right, too; they didn't seem at all pleased with me. I'd planned on sounding undecided about the whole thing until I got safely off di island; that plan was moot, now, but it wasn't my fault. There was definitely a woman to blame, and she was sitting right over there.

"What did he say?" asked Ernesto.

"He said he wasn't going to open the factory," said someone.

"What da hell..." said an angry voice.

The rusty machetes were about to come out; it was time to think, and think quickly.

"Wait a minute," I said. "So let me get this straight; you folks *want* me to open the factory?"

There was a murmuring and shouting of angry agreement.

"Oh, wow. Boy did I have everything backwards," I said. "I thought you'd probably want me to have the building torn down and get everything out of here."

"Why would we want that?" asked a man.

That was a very good question, and one that I had been desperately hoping they wouldn't ask. "Well, because...because, well," I said, bracketing my pause nicely. "Because it's an eyesore. And because if I opened it it would create pollution," I said, picking up steam. "And there'd be more and more people coming and going; you know, deliveries, shipments going out, tourists touring the rum factory, that sort of thing. I figured you'd want to keep all this unspoiled."

Everyone looked around them and at each other, as if to figure out what the hell the crazy gringo was babbling about, then the Innkeeper spoke. "You mean, dis little island, with di goats and di lizards and di fishy smell? You mean, keep all dat unspoiled?"

"Er...yes?" I said.

The Innkeeper looked at me blankly, then started laughing jovially, and soon everyone joined in, except for, I noticed, my mysterious woman who had gotten me into this mess in the first place; she simply sat quietly watching.

"Go ahead, mon; spoil it!" said the Innkeeper, who was obviously the spokesperson, at least for this lot. "If it means di people have a place to work and have money to spend, den spoil di hell out of it!"

Everyone nodded in agreement.

"Well, that changes everything," I said. Indeed it did; I wasn't dead yet, for one thing. I had to spend more time watching my mouth and less time watching exotic senoritas if I wanted to survive. "I guess I'm going to have to look at the factory more closely, then; I'll make some calls tomorrow to my financial advisers for starters and see what they have to say. Maybe I can work something out here after all. Of course, you realize this is all going to be very complicated and it may take some time. And I can't make any promises about what I'll decide to do in the end."

"How much time, do you tink?" asked the Innkeeper, somewhat suspiciously I thought.

"Oh," I said. "Maybe three or four days. And I may have to leave for a short while to go to another island and tour a rum factory. You know, to see how everything works."

The crowd turned to one another and discussed my timetable and began nodding their approval. Three days wasn't so long to wait, I heard someone say. At least he sounds willing to open the factory if he can, said another.

I'd dodged a machete this time, but I had to be more careful. I would call Gus tomorrow morning, since I didn't have any other pilot choices at hand, and schedule a flight out of here in the guise of going to check out another factory. We'd head back to Jost Van Dyke and I'd be at home in Key West within a week.

The Innkeeper grabbed me another beer; evidently I was back on the house. The woman gave me one more look before getting up and strolling away down the beach; I watched her go for as long as I could, disappointed and relieved at the same time. The music returned and people went back to talking to me and amongst themselves and I began to relax into an evening of drinking by the Caribbean ocean. It was all good now,

and I was sure I could keep myself out of trouble for
the rest of the night.

But I'd said that before. Often

"The majority of all rums are made from molasses. Molasses is the sticky residue that's left behind after boiling sugar cane juice and extracting the crystallized sugar."

Chapter 5

I awoke to a cat and several of di islanders staring down at me. The cat was perched on the back of Billy's old leather sofa; di islanders were standing in the middle of Billy's office, leaning on brooms, mops, and shovels.

"Good morning," I said from the sofa, taking a wild guess at how early it still was by using the pain in my head as a gauge.

"Good morning, boss," answered my audience, minus the cat, thankfully; it was far too AM for talking felines.

"What time is it?" I asked, attempting to sit up, then quickly abandoning the effort in hopes of keeping the room from orbiting me any faster.

"Eight o'clock, just as you said, boss," said one of the group members. "We be ready to work."

"Work?" I asked.

"Yeah, mon," said Faith, a dark skinned woman who I'd met the day before. "You told us last night to be here at eight o'clock and you'd pay us to clean di factory."

"I did? I don't remember that. And it's way too early to even think about such things. I'm sorry, but you'll have to leave; there's no work here today," I said, closing my eyes.

The crowd was silent for a moment, then I heard Ernesto, who must have been hiding in the back, say "Some of us took off work from the sugar cane fields to come here," the others grumbling their agreement.

I sensed trouble brewing again, and popped one eyelid open. "You did?" I said, becoming resigned to where this was going to end up leading.

"Yeah, mon. We did," said a particularly tall and broad shouldered dark skinned gentleman (who's name I would later learn was Jedidiah) who didn't look very happy with me at all.

"Maybe the place could use a good cleaning," I said quickly, scanning the room with my one open lid like Popeye. "Only eight hours of work though today, alright?" I had some money on me, or did yesterday, when I'd arrived. But I was obviously going to have to find a way to get more cash, and soon.

"Eight hours? Cool, boss," said a happy looking man. "Rodrigo always makes us work for twelve hours at his fields."

"Well, I'm not Rodrigo," I said. "Boss needs to sleep some more now," I added, closing my eye. Again I didn't hear any sounds of movement, other than the cat licking himself, so I opened the other eye to give the first one a well deserved break. No one had moved, and they were still standing staring at me. "Yes?" I said.

"Do you want us to go to work now, boss?" asked the big man.

"Yes! Please! Thank you!" I said, exasperated.

"Okay," he said, and everyone began shuffling out of the room, except Ernesto.

"Yes, Ernesto?" I said.

"What about tomorrow?" said Ernesto. "Will there be work then, too?"

I sighed. "I don't know. Let's see how it goes today first, shall we? Then we'll talk about it."

"Okay, senor," he said, and turned to leave.

I closed my eye again but heard the sound of sweeping next to me, then sneezed hard as a cloud of dust flew into my nose. I sat up and found Faith sweeping the floor.

"I'll clean up di office first; you shouldn't have to sleep in such a dirty room, mon," she said.

I was going to tell her that I hadn't planned to sleep here at all and would have sworn that I talked to the Innkeeper about a room at the motel, but decided to give arguing and sleep up for the moment. Instead I stood up unsteadily and walked out and through the main factory, followed by my cat, making our way to the patio where I found a lovely, ratty looking lounger to collapse upon.

This had already turned into a rather expensive day; it was just past eight and I already had a headache, a cat, and a ten person staff that I hadn't had when I arrived yesterday. But I couldn't really say no to them (well the cat, maybe); besides the facts that I didn't want to get fed to the sharks and was so hungover I would have paid them to simply go away, I didn't remember anything past my third beer and sixth rum I had eventually and obviously unwisely switched to. It was more than possible I'd been talked into hiring a cleaning crew today; it may have even been my idea, given what a good mood and state I'd been in.

I felt like just laying there in the shade all day, or perhaps paying one of my new employees mucho dinero to make a run to Monkey Drool's for a Bloody Mary or three. But I also felt terribly grungy and unless my mystery woman from yesterday strolled past and offered to clean *me*, I was liable to continue to feel like crap until I got moving. And that big, blue ocean spreading out in front of me looked mighty inviting for a dip.

So I hooked up a mental crane and with some difficulty managed to lift myself out of the chair and into a more or less upright position for the second time today. Then I stumbled down towards the beach, my feline friend still in tow. I didn't know why I'd been adopted by said calico so quickly, but like most of di islanders and cats I'd met in my life I was sure he had a motive behind it; perhaps there was a tuna cannery somewhere on di island he wanted me to look into.

When we got down next to the gently rolling waters, I realized I didn't have my swimsuit with me. But I figured I wasn't exactly standing on a private beach at the Hilton, either. For all I knew, I owned this plot of sand, too. So I stripped down to my boxers and waded into the cool ocean, the cat choosing to stay behind and chase sand crabs.

I felt better immediately, and even more so when I got out far enough to duck entirely under the surface. The water was crystal clear, and I could see colorful little fish darting about in their world that I was visiting. I swam around for a bit, letting the salt water wash away the night.

It wasn't the first time in my life I'd been in the ocean, but it was a totally different experience. I was alone, except for my feline friend, as opposed to being one of a hundred tourists crammed onto a beach somewhere. The waters here seemed unspoiled, and I couldn't help feeling that mother nature was still happy to be here and share her space with me.

I would have loved to splash around like a sea otter for a few hours, but after too short a while my stomach began pointing out that it hadn't had anything to chew on for a goodly number of hours. I seemed to recall eating some sort of food-like substance at some point last night, but I couldn't say what and when. I was running on empty again now, and I knew I'd better appease my tummy grumblings before it started eating itself, so I reluctantly left the water as my ancient ancestors had so unwisely done eons ago.

I put my clothes back on, which left me with an uncomfortably wet inner lining, but I wasn't about to go gallivanting around in my skivvies, no matter how secluded di island seemed. I trudged back up the hill and went around to the front of the factory hoping I'd be able to sneak away before incurring any more costs this morning, just as an old panel truck pulled up. Two men wearing coveralls got out and met me before I could make a dash for open ground.

"Are you Billy's nephew?" asked one of the men.

I sighed. "Yes, I am," I said. "And you two are..."

"...here to fix di roof," said the other man.

"I had a feeling you were going to say something like that," I said. "Be my guest."

Step one, go find breakfast.

Step two, figure out how to get more cash.

Step three, call Gus before I went broke.

It was becoming a busy morning.

"Sailors in the British Navy were given Grog, made from water, lime juice, and rum. Pirates favored Bomboo, made from water, sugar, nutmeg, and rum."

Chapter 6

Breakfast was easily marked off on my checklist; I asked the roofers where sustenance might be found and they pointed me down the road towards the center of di island. It seemed there was a street system of sorts in place, with four main dirt roads that went more or less to the north, south, east, and west portions of di island, intersecting roughly in the center. That area was known as the Crossroads, and a handful of small businesses were gathered there, such as a market and a cantina. And a bank.

It wasn't that bad a walk, about a mile or so, and it gave me a chance to get a good look at di island, or at least the western side of it. It really was a beautiful place, very lush, and you couldn't argue with the climate as long as you weren't a die hard hockey fan. The people I met along the way were unfailingly friendly; there were no odd stares today, and I guessed that word had probably gotten around to everyone by now who the stranger in their midst was.

I had a nice island breakfast at the cantina consisting of eggs, fried plantains, sausage, and red beans. It was a bit heavier than what I was used to, but it was tasty and I felt good having it in my belly. It got me ready to face the rest of the day and whatever else was going to come my way, which was good since I knew there was bound to be more.

I couldn't raise Gus on my cell; I just kept getting a message that his phone was unavailable at this time. Not surprising given his on the move occupation, and I wasn't sure how good the phone service was in this part of the Caribbean, either. I hoped he would fly into range some time soon, though; I needed to set up a ride out of paradise and back to paradise as soon as possible, if that made any sense.

I went into the tiny bank and found that I could transfer funds to it from my account stateside. Mr. Wonbago was there, in charge; obviously he was a man of many suit jackets, and he suggested I open a business account if I was going to have employees on my payroll. I tried explaining to him that I didn't *have* a payroll, but he didn't seem to believe me. I wasn't sure I believed me either, given the twelve people working for me at the factory right now. But I held fast and managed to leave the building with more money on the way, and a pamphlet for a 3rd Bank of di island Business Friendly Savers Account in my back pocket, courtesy of Wonbago.

By this time it was pushing towards noon. I was actually tempted to go back to the factory and see how things were coming along, and had to remind myself that I didn't care how things were coming along; I was basically paying to keep the workers busy while I tried to work my way out of this mess and maybe have some fun in the process. I understood their point of view, of course. They wanted a good place to work; very natural. I just wasn't ready to be the one to provide it for them. I hated bosses and had no desire to turn into one.

"Hey, laddie; come here, mon."

I was standing in the middle of the intersection at the Crossroads, trying to figure what to do and which direction to go next, when a man called out to me from the shade of the porch jutting out from the market. I walked over to him and found he was sitting at a small wooden table, dominoes scattered across it.

"Do you play?" he asked, indicating the dominoes.

"No, I never have," I said. "I watched some men play in Jamaica but I couldn't pick up the rules, other than matching the ends."

"Sit down, mon. I'll teach ya," he said. "It's easy. Here, have a soda." He handed me a cold bottle of Ting, a tasty grapefruit soda I'd also had in Jamaica, and I took it, then sat down across from him. I had nothing better to do at the moment than to try my hand at rolling dem bones.

"Thanks for the drink," I said. "My name is-"

"I know who you are, Jack," he said with a big smile. "Di whole island knows who *you* are by now," he added, confirming my earlier suspicions.

"I guess I'm not surprised," I said. "I bet news travels fast on an island this size."

"Faster than it happens, sometimes," he said with a laugh.

"And you?" I said. "What's your name?"

"I be Roger," he said. "But everyone calls me Jolly Roger."

Over the next couple of hours I learned two things. One, I suck at dominoes. And two, Roger definitely deserved his nickname; he was one of the most amiable and happy individuals I'd ever met. He was thirty some years old, dark and stocky with a good Irish potato belly, having been born in Jamaica to a Jamaican father and an Irish mother. His head sported dreadlocks and his wide grin several gold teeth, made from melted down Spanish doubloons, or so he said. Roger's dialect didn't seem overly concerned with choosing between his nationalities, and many a sentence from his lips would end up as a sort of word gumbo, such as *"Look at di lady over der, laddie; now dat be one bonnie lass!",* and it only added to his colorful nature.

Jolly Roger was captain of the Crustacean, one of the fishing boats I had seen in the harbor yesterday upon my arrival. Crusty, as he called her, was out of service at the moment, and he was waiting for a part to arrive to get her engine running again. He didn't seem very put out over missing a couple days of work, and as laid back as he was I had a hard time picturing him being overly concerned about much of anything.

We played dominoes and talked in the warm shade as time moved along at an island pace, slowly but surely. Occasionally someone would stop and watch for a while but they soon moved on, probably bored by my pathetic skills. When I finished losing my sixth match in a row I ran up the white flag, and Roger and I sat back to chat over a couple more of the delicious Tings I'd ducked into the market to buy.

"How did you become a sea captain?" I asked Roger. "Was it because of your father?"

"Aye, laddie," he said. "He be di one responsible, dat be for sure."

"He was a captain, too?" I asked.

"No, he be an insurance salesman," said Roger. "I see him trudge home from work every day in Jamaica and I tell meself, mon, no way dat ever be I. So I head to di sea and now here I be on dis crazy island."

"Cool story," I said. He seemed like a particularly honest and straightforward person to me, and I needed someone to talk to about my current situation. "So tell me something, Roger; what do you think about me and this rum factory I find myself with?"

"What do you mean?" he said.

"Well, everyone else around here seems to have some pretty robust opinions about it," I said.

"Ah, been feelin' a little pushed around, haven't ya laddie?" said Roger with a mischievous grin.

"You could say that, yeah," I said. "I was just wondering what your opinion is."

"My opinion is dat it's your factory and your life; do with both what you be wantin', mon," said Roger. "Don't do something ya don't want to do just because they want ya to do it."

"So you're not planning to try and talk me into reopening it, or show up and fix the roof whether I asked you to or not?" I said.

"No way, mon; it's not my business. In fact, if me boat was running and you wanted to leave, I'd give you a ride home right this minute," said Roger. "It would just take a while; Crusty's not the fastest boat in di sea."

"Just out of curiosity, when is your engine part supposed to get here?" I asked, thinking it might be good to have a backup escape plan, no matter how slow it might be. Who knew how long it would take to get a hold of Gus or how long it would be before Crazy Chester washed up on shore.

"The part will get here whenever Gus get's around to delivering it," said Roger.

"Him again," I said with a sigh.

"Ya, mon; Gus is FedEx, American Airlines, and Santa all rolled into one unreliable SOB," said Roger with a chuckle.

"Oh, well. Guess I'm not in that big a hurry to leave," I said. I got up from my chair reluctantly; it had been a pleasant couple of hours, but I needed to get back to the bank and pick up my incoming money so I could pay the employees I didn't have for the work I didn't want them to do. "Is it safe to walk around with a lot of cash?" I asked Roger. "I'm still undecided about my Business Friendly Savers Account."

"Aye, it be safe, mon. We don't have crime here, laddie," said Roger. "No one will bother ya, I can promise you, dat. Especially, you; no one wants to upset di new owner of di rum factory."

"That's an upside, at least," I said. "Thanks for the games; even though you beat the heck out of me, it was fun. Maybe we can play again before I leave, *if* I leave."

"No problem, laddie," said Roger. "If you're here long enough you might even win a game."

I hoped I wasn't going to be here *that* long.

"Where there is a sea, there be pirates."-Greek Proverb

Chapter 7

When I got back to the factory I was impressed by how much my non-employees had gotten done. It was much cleaner inside; all of the refuse had been removed, and anything useful, like aging casks, had been dusted off and rolled and stacked neatly on one side. The workman were still hammering away up on the roof; not surprising given all the holes that it had. But the birds had been chased out at least, so maybe my cat had even put in some time.

The place still needed a helluva lot of work, however. The cleaning had actually revealed that even more; it just didn't look like a dump site now. A good portion of the hanging light fixtures were gone for example, having fallen to the floor, their support brackets rusted in the salt air. The floor was in pretty bad shape, too, the concrete eroded away in places either due to time or a poorly done job in the first place.

Billy's old office was neat and tidy and in good shape though, thanks to Faith; even the mattress on the bed seemed dust free, perhaps from a good beating. Not that I was ready to sleep there again. I had no idea how I'd gotten here last night, and barring any repeat blackout drunk performances I had no intention of ending up here this evening. But it was good to know that if I did choose to do a spontaneous encore that I'd have a nice, spic and span room to wake up from it in.

At least the factory now looked like it might be worth a little something after all, and perhaps when I got back stateside I could contact someone who worked internationally to sell the place for me. If di islanders were lucky it would be someone who wanted to open their own business, rum factory or otherwise.

When five o'clock rolled around my staff gathered outside to get paid, and I gave each of them a little something extra for a job well done and to buy me some good will. They all seemed pretty ecstatic about the deal, and I got the feeling that what I'd given them was a fair amount of money on di island. The roofers hadn't finished the repairs yet so I told them to come back again tomorrow, as well as a couple of the men who said they were carpenters and offered to fix the broken window shutters. The rest of my staff stood looking at me with puppy dog eyes, so being a sap I told them they could come back too and clean up the yard and patio.

Thus being assured of spending a nice chunk of change again tomorrow (I tried to look at it as an investment, although I wasn't sure in what yet), I agreed to meet everyone later at Monkey Drool's for some fresh Grouper sandwiches they were going to grill up on the beach, and rounds of free drinks they promised to buy me now that they were all rich. I told myself I could go as long as I agreed to behave this time, but promises made to yourself aren't very useful since you hardly mind when the promisee ends up breaking them, and it's damned hard to even get an apology afterwards.

Which is the only thing close to an excuse I can come up with for donning the monkey's sombrero and eye patch, and while tightly holding on to my sixth coconut mug of Pickled Parrot Punch, limboing as low as I could go in my skivvies.

Someone should do a study on why beaches are so damned intoxicating; I'd be glad to participate as a test subject. It's just sand and water, nothing all that exotic, and each of them by themselves are pretty harmless. But take almost any down in the dumps human being and plop them where the agua meets the land and soon they'll be as happy as a teenage boy at a women's gymnastic meet (well, almost as happy, anyway).

As for my own current case of madness (and this wasn't the first time I'd come down with the fever), it hadn't set in immediately. I'd made my way over to Monkey Drool's and Ernesto had bought me a cerveza, and then Faith bought me another. More and more people arrived, including Cavin, and we all joked and chatted and had a nice conversation. No one talked much about the factory, just a few anecdotes about the old rum days, for which I was grateful; I didn't feel like I was under any kind of pressure other than to simply enjoy myself.

Soon Jolly Roger showed up with a cooler of fish and a grill, and before long delicious Grouper sandwiches were being passed through the crowd. The Innkeeper broke out something he called Pickled Parrot Punch, Cavin broke out his guitar, a long haired gringo named Boyd broke out his bongos, and somehow my shirt and shorts soon went awol and I found myself looking up at a bamboo stick.

I wasn't any better at limbo than I'd been at dominoes, since I'm about as limber as the Tin Man standing in a tsunami. I might have done a bit better if I'd set my drink down, but I steadfastly refused to let it out of my tender loving care. I was hardly worried about my performance anyway; each time I'd lose my balance I'd just collapse on my back in the sand and giggle, acting like either a total idiot or the wisest person on Earth, depending on the stuffiness level of your personality.

I got up out of the sand again, and Faith brushed off my back. She wasn't being flirty; in fact, it turned out she was married to Ernesto.

"How did I do that time?" I said.

"You almost made it, mon," said Faith.

"Aye, if ye didn't have a head it would have been almost close," said Roger with a smile. "You might want to lose the sombrero, though."

"Never!" I said. "It's far too stylish."

"If ya say so, mon," said Roger.

"I have to pee," I announced, noticing suddenly that it should be my top priority and changing the subject just as suddenly.

"Di bathroom has a long line," said the Innkeeper, as he walked by with another tray of PPP's. It wasn't hard to tell he was in a good mood, too; many of my dollars were ending up in his pocket tonight. "I would just walk down di beach if I were you," he said.

That seemed like a sensible suggestion, and I wandered off away from the fire and along the sea. I came to an old fishing boat, broken in half, that was pulled up on shore, and figured it was as good a place as any to do my business since it provided some cover. I'd just finished when a voice came from down by the ocean.

"Dangerous waters be these, lad; beware."

I jumped. Almost, at least; I was too sedated and relaxed to actually manage much more than a mild twitch. I peered in the direction from which said voice had come, and saw, for the second time in as many days, a pirate, standing with his back to me.

I made sure I got a better look at him this time; that was definitely a tri-cornered hat over the top of his long, greyish hair, those were puffy sleeves, and those be tall, leather boots with a cuff; yep, he was a pirate, alright. I didn't see any weapons, however; perhaps he'd been marooned here like me but had lost his pistol with the one shot.

"Hey," I said to him, hardly the best pirate greeting of all time, and I spent most of the next day wishing I'd hit him back with a hearty *"Avast!"* instead.

"Many a brave sailor has been taken down to Davy Jones in these shoals," he said, not turning and seemingly unperturbed by my hey.

"Well, I just came down here to pee, so I think I'll be okay," I said.

"Jest all ye want," he said gruffly. "On a night like this be ye thankful ye stand on the shore."

I looked up at the sky for storms and found it filled with more stars than fish in the sea, then gazed in front of me at the calm ocean playfully teasing the sand. "Everything looks pretty calm to me," I said.

"Ye be warned, matey," he said, turning slowly and moving away down the beach.

"Yes, but about what?" I said.

"Beware," he said.

"If you say so," I said. I watched him go for a while, until suddenly he seemed to disappear into thin air. I shook my head; the Pickled Parrots were obviously punching me harder than I thought, then walked back to Monkey Drool's.

I sat down next to Ernesto and Roger up near the bar, and eyed my drink suspiciously. "What's in this thing, anyway?" I asked.

"It's top secret," said Ernesto. "If you found out the Innkeeper would have to kill you."

"Funny; they have that one down here too, do they?" I said.

Ernesto looked at me very seriously.

"You were kidding, right?" I said, taking nothing for granted.

"I don't know, senor. When Damon the Chicken Man figured out what was the secret ingredient in the Innkeeper's first drink, the Big Banana, he mysteriously disappeared," said Ernesto.

"Dat's because he moved to Texas," said Roger.

"Oh; I didn't know that," said Ernesto. "Never mind, then."

"So what was the secret ingredient?" I asked.

"Banana," said Ernesto and Roger together.

"Ah," I said.

"But why did you want to know what was in the drink?" asked Ernesto.

"Because I just had a strange conversation with a pirate down the beach," I said. "I thought maybe the

Innkeeper was spiking these things with the sort of hallucinogenic Uncle Billy might have played with."

Roger and Ernesto stared at me, then Roger said, in a hushed voice, "He saw di ghost."

"Ghost?" I said. "What ghost?"

"The ghost of Captain Black Dog," said Ernesto.

"Oh, seriously..." I said.

"It's true, laddie," said Roger. "Di legends say Captain Black Dog pirated these waters centuries ago, until his ship crashed into a reef off di island during a storm, all hands lost."

"Really," I said, in my best but rusty, big city cynical tone.

"Si. Now he walks di island in search of the treasure they say he buried here," said Ernesto.

"A bit absent minded, was he?" I said, still not believing a word of it. "I mean, if he's the one who buried it..."

"Ya, well, it's probably not easy bein' a ghost," said Roger with an evil grin.

"You know, I saw him yesterday afternoon, too, in the inside bar," I said.

"Aye, he often sits in di dark, tinking about his lost crew. Sometimes you'll hear a sea shanty coming through di wall," said Roger.

"Uh huh. I still think you guys are full of it, but it was a great story," I said. "And while we're on the subject of mysterious people, who was that beautiful woman I saw here yesterday afternoon? Or was she just another ghost?"

"You mean dat bonnie lass over der?" asked Roger, pointing towards the beach.

I looked, and there she was, next to the fire, illuminated in its amber glow as she danced to Cavin's guitar. I watched her slowly swaying in the flickering light and swallowed hard. "Yep," I squeaked. "That would be the one."

I took off my eye patch so I could have the use of both my lenses. Between her and the ghost of Captain Black Dog, I was finding her the harder one to believe was real. Tall and dark and mature and lovely, if the gal from Ipanema stood next to her she'd just be messing up the view. And if everyone else was like me, the men *she* passed wouldn't go *ah*, they'd be struck speechless.

"Who is she?" I said.

"Why don't you go ask her, mon?" suggested Roger.

"Are you kidding? That'd be like walking over and asking Beyonce to dance," I said. Come to think about it, that was who she was reminding me of, especially the way she was bumping to Boyd's bongo beats in her red bikini and sheer yellow sarong.

"Who is Beyonce?" asked Ernesto.

"You need to get out more," I said. "Look, you guys might as well just tell me who she is now while it will still do me some good, because I can guarantee I'm not going do it myself until I drink about ten more of these things, and by then I won't remember what she said anyway."

"Dat be Isabella Vaccaria," said Roger. "She be di most beautiful lassie on di island."

"Yeah, that much I figured out for myself," I said. "And she's married to..."

"No one," said Ernesto.

"Then she's dating..." I said.

"No one," said Roger.

"Why?" I said. "Are all the men here crazy?"

Roger shrugged. "Don't know. I tink it's because she hasn't found di right man, mon. Not so many people here since di rum days ended." He watched me watching her for a moment, then said "Maybe you be di right mon, you tink?"

"Me? I'm never the right mon, er man. At least not with anyone like that," I said.

"You never know until you try," said Ernesto.

"Maybe, but I can take a pretty educated guess," I said. "She's just way out of my league. I mean, look at her. She's...she's...oh, hell. She's going to limbo now, isn't she?"

"Aye," said Roger, grinning.

"I need a drink," I said.

"But you have a drink, senor," said Ernesto.

"Then I need two drinks; one for each hand and eyeball," I said.

Faith came up and sat down next to Ernesto. "Why di boss look so glum?" she asked.

"Isabella," said Roger.

"Ah," said Faith. "I should have known di look,"

I watched Isabella shimmy towards the bamboo staff two of di islanders were holding, already far lower than anything I had attempted and failed. Then she bent way back and slowly and sinuously slid beneath it with ease.

"She's awfully good at that, isn't she?" I said, gulping.

"Si," said Ernesto dreamily, eliciting a playful slap on the cheek from Faith.

"I can't go nearly that low and I don't have her extra, um, altitudes to deal with," I said.

"Well, boss, if you like her very much, maybe if you open di factory she will see you be a man of property," said Faith.

"Maybe," I said. I had to admit, if I thought it would truly help, I'd be sorely tempted to become a rum tycoon right that minute. But I couldn't imagine her falling for anyone less than the rich, famous, or powerful, and I didn't think that kicking out a few bottles of pirate pleasure would put me in any of those categories, except maybe with the pirates themselves. "I get the feeling she might want something more."

"But you be a nice man, too; dat goes a long way with di ladies," said Faith.

"I tell you, if that's true on di island, there are probably about a million American guys who'll be wanting to immigrate here," I said. "But just in case you're right I'll keep being nice and buy the next round of drinks."

I went up to the bar and did so, then sat and talked to the Innkeeper, ignoring Isabella for a while so I could cool myself down, and when I looked back later she was gone.

It was just as well; I had enough problems already, what with being stranded on a beautiful tropical island with a bunch of overly friendly people who thought I should make rum in the Caribbean for a living,

I spent the night wondering if I might be looking at things all wrong, before my ninth mug of Pickled Parrot Punch set in and my brain said adios for the evening.

"Ernest Hemingway spent many years writing and drinking rum in Havana, Cuba, and loved both mojitos and daiquiris."

Chapter 8

I opened my eyes and thought, "Not again," and made a mental note to try and have some idea how I got to where I was one of these mornings. This time, I was lying in a hammock, but other than that, I had no clue once more.

The hammock was stretched between two palm trees, and the palm trees were in a fenced in yard that had been meticulously landscaped; every flower, fern and stone seemed to have been placed just so. A small, clear pond with a tinkling fountain resided in one corner, and what I guessed to be papayas and mangos grew in another. Small colorful birds happily twittered and flitted about in the branches of the trees, and butterflies did the same amongst the bevy of flowers peppered about the yard. Wherever the heck I was, it was beautiful, like a paradise inside of paradise.

I managed to get out of the hammock without any comic ejections onto the ground, and walked over to the table and chairs that sat on a stone patio off the back of the small house that owned the yard. I found a picnic basket and a hand drawn map of where I was on di island, along with a note that read *"Gone to work at the factory, boss; help yourself to breakfast,"* and it was signed, Ernesto and Faith.

So this was Ernesto and Faith's home, unless they were in the habit of delivering picnic breakfasts to passed out gringos wherever they might be. Now that I knew where I was I vaguely remembered a few of us coming back here after Monkey Drool's closed last night for a nightcap or three. That made me feel better; at least I'd been invited and hadn't climbed over a wall and made myself at home in someone's back yard. Now if just once I could make it back to a bed at the motel like I'd been planning to I'd be golden.

I opened the picnic basket and found fruit, banana bread, and mango juice, and sat down to eat. As I munched the delicious meal I found myself feeling a little guilty, like I hadn't done enough to pay back how friendly and kind everyone had been since my arrival on di island. Especially since I had no intention of opening the factory at this point, and was sort of receiving all these little perks on false pretenses. I told myself I didn't know what I expected us to do; between yesterday and today we were handing out all sorts of green paper kindnesses out of our pockets, which was pretty damned nice of us, too, I thought, if a bit impersonal.

After I finished eating I left the property by a side gate. Guided by the map, I made my way down a small, winding path through the thick trees that surrounded the house, and eventually found the main road and headed south towards the Crossroads. I dug through my pockets as I walked and was relieved to find I still had my cell phone, and turned it on. I was surprised when it showed it was already almost one in the afternoon; either I'd been really tired or had really tied one on again last night, or both. I gave Gus a quick try and couldn't get through as I'd expected, and that was the last call I was going to make for a while as my phone battery went completely dead.

I thought about my situation as I walked under the hot sun towards the Crossroads, and decided that things weren't all that bad. So I couldn't get a hold of Gus; big deal. He'd have to show up eventually, if for no other reason than to deliver Roger's boat engine part, and then I'd go home. In the mean time I had to admit I was enjoying myself, and if I did have a problem to worry about, that was the one; I was beginning to kind of like it here.

Of course I liked it back in Key West, too, and I wasn't ready to just chuck all that aside; going from wintery Minnesota to the sunny Keys had had its obvious advantages. But going from the Keys to di island, well that would be a different sort of change.

Living in Key West wasn't all that different from living in a city anywhere else in the United States; it just had more of the good things, like sunshine, food, music, and too many great bars to even visit in a day. And all of it in a quirky, laid back, tropical atmosphere. But living here on di island would be almost like living in the past, when things were simpler. Something akin to medieval times, except with plumbing and electricity, and without tyrannical kings and the plague; kind of a tropical renaissance festival. I wasn't sure I could do without some of the modern comforts I wouldn't be able to get here, like movies and pizza delivery.

Still, di island definitely had it's appeal. As I strolled along I noticed how quiet is was, for instance. There were no cars going by, no one working on the street. There wasn't a crowd of people around me like there usually was in Key West. It was just myself, the birds and the bees, and the occasional passerby. It was intensely peaceful, if that was possible adjective wise, and if the whole thing didn't seem so far fetched I might seriously consider moving here and opening the factory.

But I didn't know the first thing about making rum, as shocking as that seemed. I'd tried to brew beer once, but it ended up tasting like Nyquil, and I guessed that distilling rum was probably even harder. And I'd have to figure out how to make money at it, too. *Importing* ingredients, *exporting* the product, *marketing* the rum; there were just too many *tings* involved. Sticking with just drinking the rum instead, which I was already accomplished at, seemed much simpler and much less stressful.

Besides, when I tried actually posing the question to myself just for the heck of it, it made the idea seem even more ludicrous; should Jack move to a tiny island in the Caribbean and rehabilitate a run down factory and make rum? It wasn't the sort of thing you usually asked yourself, and it just sounded silly. How could I seriously consider doing a thing when thinking about the thing almost made me giggle out loud.

I came to a small cemetery by the side of the road and put my musings aside for the moment. I wondered if Billy was buried there; given the small size of di island I figured the chances were good. So I pushed open the white picket fence gate and went inside.

I wandered around for some time, checking marker after marker with no luck, until I came to a plot with a new and simple wooden gravestone that read *"Captain Billy Danielson, 1949-2011."* It felt odd standing on this far away Caribbean soil knowing that buried beneath the ground in front of my feet was my dad's brother. And that he was my uncle and this was the closest the two of us had ever come to meeting one another. I wasn't getting all weepy eyed; as I said, we'd never even met. But a series of events starting with Billy and my father had led me to be standing on this exact spot, and I was trying to give it it's due, whatever it's due might have been.

"He was a good man, your uncle."

I looked and found an old, Latin looking gentleman I hadn't noticed before sitting on a nearby bench under a tree. "You knew him?" I said, walking towards him.

"I did," he said. "Sit down and I will tell you about him. My name is Luis." I did so, and he said, "Billy was a good man. A little strange, perhaps, but then who isn't?"

"What was he like?" I said.

"Billy was quiet, and a dreamer; he came down to di island to get away from people. He had tried to do the same thing in the north woods of Canada, but he said it was way too damned cold," said Luis.

"How did he end up with a rum factory?" I said. "My father told me he was kind of a flake; how did he ever come up with the money?"

"Now that is a good question," said Luis. "Nobody knows for sure. But Billy did have a boat; that's why people called him Captain Billy. And Billy took his boat to Jamaica many times, and then to Key West."

"So he did return to the states after all," I said.

"Yes, but I'm not sure the states ever knew he was back," said Luis. "I don't think he ever made it official."

"Then what was he doing there?" I said.

"Stopping in Jamaica? And then over to Key West? Back in those days?" said Luis. "What do you think he was doing?"

"You mean, he was running grass?" I said, incredulously.

"Well, there is no proof, but he got all that money somewhere," said Luis.

"That's something I bet my father never knew," I said with a chuckle. "So why didn't he ever open the factory? He didn't get caught, did he?"

"No, his boat sank," said Luis. "All his money was tied up in the factory by then, and without his boat he was never able to get enough funds together to finish what he had started."

I'd come for a story, and I certainly had a good one to tell now. "One thing I still don't get it; why did Billy even bother with a factory if he had all that marijuana money? He doesn't sound like the type that would even want his own business, and he could have lived forever here with all the cash he must have spent trying to get it open."

"He did it for you, Jack," said Luis.

"For me?" I said. "What are you talking about; we didn't even know one another."

"Perhaps. But he began to take his responsibilities as your uncle very seriously," said Luis. "Do you remember the time your father was in the car crash when you were young?"

"How could I forget? He almost died," I said. "It was the scariest week of my life."

"Well, Billy heard about it afterwards; I don't know how. But it made him think. As your godfather, if anything happened to your parents you would have been his responsibility," said Luis.

"I doubt that; I'm sure my grandparents would have taken care of me. Which would have been a real hoot, by the way," I said.

"Maybe. But Billy decided he wanted something to give to you in any case."

"A rum factory," I said. "How did he ever expect to pull that off, anyway? I'm guessing he didn't know much more about making rum than me."

"No, he didn't. But I did," said Luis.

"You?" I said.

"Yes. I was born in Cuba, and my father made rum, and his father made rum, and his father's father made rum. I was going to make rum, too, in Cuba, and my parents sent me to the states to learn modern chemistry and business, but not before my father taught me everything he knew. I got stuck in America when Cuba changed because of that bastard Castro, and I never went back. But I did make rum for many years all over the islands," said Luis.

"And then you met Billy, and I bet he had a proposition for you," I said.

"Yes," said Luis. "And soon I was stuck here with nothing to do. Not that I'm complaining; I could have left, but for some reason I couldn't leave the factory behind. And the years here have been good."

"At least some of it makes some sort of sense now," I said. "Although why Billy chose a rum factory as a way to show some responsibility as my uncle is beyond me. Hadn't he ever heard of savings bonds?"

"Ah, now that part was just Billy being Billy," said Luis. "As I said, Billy liked rum and he loved the idea of making his own. And he loved di island. So he wanted to give all that to you. When we look at other people we often see them as reflections of ourselves, with the same wants and dreams. And Billy didn't even know you so it was easy for him to imagine you would love the same things as he did."

I looked around me at the beautiful tropical surroundings; Billy did have a nice place to spend eternity in. "I suppose it's hard to understand someone not wanting to live in a place like this."

"Oh, not so hard," said Luis. "After I was done with my four years of school in Miami I was tempted to stay. There was so much to do, so much variety, and it was so exciting! But on the mainland I did sometimes miss the peace and quiet you find in a place like this. And

I missed knowing I wouldn't be shot at in any given moment. So I came back to the Caribbean."

"It would be something to own a little house here, and to just get out of bed and walk over to the factory. Drink some good local coffee on the patio while I looked out at the ocean. And then go inside and make me some rum." I took the time to imagine it all; the serenity and simplicity of such a life, then shook my head. "It's insane, though. I have a life I'm quite fond of already and I still don't know a thing about making rum. Unless-"

"Yes? Unless what, Jack?" asked Luis.

"Unless you were looking for a job," I said.

"It's been years since I worked in the trade, and I'm an old man now," said Luis.

"I understand," I said, almost disappointed, even though I wasn't sure I was being serious anyway.

"But the rum, it never leaves your blood. And in all my years I never had the opportunity to make *my* rum; I have always worked under someone else," said Luis quietly. "That's what your uncle Billy promised to get me to come here in the first place, that I could make my own rum blends at last."

"So if I fell farther off my rocker than I already have and decided to go through with this madness, you'd be interested in being my brew master?"

"In the rum trade the title is Master Blender. But to answer your question, yes, I would be interested. To spend your whole life devoting it to one art but to never create your own masterpiece would be like a great painter who painted nothing but forgeries," said Luis.

I stood up. "Well, I seriously doubt if I'm going to stay and do this, but it's good to know I'd have someone with me who knows about rum," I said. "And I'd love to make your dream come true, but I have to decide if it's my dream, too."

"Of course," said Luis. "We all must do what we must do."

"I'm not so sure of that anymore. Billy didn't have to build the factory, and if he hadn't, I wouldn't be standing here on di island even considering finishing it," I said. "Lately I've taken a road that's a little less traveled than most, but the one Billy was on is even more deserted, and I'm afraid to take that off-ramp. Maybe some day I'd be able to find the nerve but by then it would be too late."

"It would be tragic to look back years from now and know that you missed out on something special," said Luis.

"Yes, it would," I said. "One of the things I recently promised myself was that when something cool, intriguing, or tasty presented itself I would go ahead and buy it, do it, or eat it, whenever possible, so I wouldn't have any pangs of regret later. But this; this is cool, intriguing *and* tasty, but on such a huge life changing scale. I just don't know..."

"Then it seems you have a lot to think about, Jack," said Luis.

I did indeed.

"I pity them greatly, but I must be mum. For how could we do without sugar and rum?" -William Cowper

Chapter 9

I decided it was way past time to get myself organized. I was still wearing the same clothes as the day I'd arrived for starters, and despite the fact they had spent a good portion of their stay on di island without me in them, they were beginning to get a tad bit gamey. As was I; I didn't know what the odds were of finding a hot shower on di island, but one sounded damned good by now.

So I set out on a quest to find my long lost luggage. The last place I remembered seeing it was at Monkey Drool's, and I went and talked to the Innkeeper and found that he'd been storing my bags for me in a room at the Coconut Motel, in case I ever felt like sleeping where I'd paid him to be able to. I gave him some more money for yet another night's stay, hoping I'd actually use it this time, and he gave me a key and I went to the room.

My luggage was indeed there, patiently waiting for me. The room itself was simple, with painted white slatted walls and wooden floors, and furnished with a bed, dresser, and table and chairs. But it was clean and had a bathroom, although I had to settle for a cold shower, which was refreshing never the less. After scouring myself spotless I dug out my charger and plugged in my phone, then laid down on the bed to relax and think. I got as far as *"What's the problem now, Jack?"* before quickly passing out.

After a two hour rather ferocious cat nap I woke up and checked my phone and found I had a text from Crazy Chester saying he'd be arriving on di island this afternoon, and to meet him over at Monkey Drool's. That put me on a pressing time table; if I wanted a ride home with Chester to my Keys I'd have to come to a decision about the factory very quickly. And meeting him at Monkey Drool's also meant my mind would probably be a goner shortly after arriving and I'd lose all my powers of contemplation for those hours as well; I needed to get my ass and brain moving, and quickly.

So I hurried back again to the factory; it was close to four-thirty and payroll time by now, and my workers would be busily wrapping up another day of not being employed by me. Everyone got some more of my money that could have gone towards mojitos in Key West, but at least no one asked about work for the following day; it was Friday, and the weekend was still the weekend on di island, and it was close to five o'clock right here.

After everyone left I wandered around my property for a while, since it was at the center of my debate. I had to admit that even though I wasn't sure it mattered, it was amazing how much better the place looked. The roof and window shutters seemed fully bird and weather proof now, and the yard and patio were much improved. I never would have thought looking at it two days ago it was even salvageable, but though it still needed work and tender loving care it now showed potential.

I went into Billy's office and puttered around, checking out the old photos and brick-a-brac on the walls and shelves. I couldn't tell for sure if there were any pictures of Billy or not, since I didn't know what he looked like. But I did find an old black and white of two young boys taken in front of Yankee Stadium, and I figured it was most likely of the two brothers, Billy and my dad. There was also a picture in which I recognized Luis posing next to one of the shiny new stills, taken back in the rum days.

There was an awful lot of junk crammed onto the shelves, and I inspected as much of it as I could. I wanted to try and make some sense of my uncle, and you can often tell a lot about a person by their things. Billy's clutter told me he was sentimental, just by saving and displaying so much stuff. There was a very old train ticket from Minneapolis to Toronto, and I wondered if it was from the day Billy had left America to avoid the draft. A small woman's pendant hung draped over a piece of driftwood, alongside a menu from a restaurant in Belize; souvenirs from a memorable date perhaps. And there also was a large dog collar with a gold tag that read "*Sammy*", probably from an old pet.

I didn't know for sure why I was bothering to try and learn more about Billy; on the one hand he seemed to be just a crazy old hippie who happened to be my Dad's brother. On the other hand though, for some reason I seemed to mean something to him, enough to cause him to build the factory I was standing in right now. In a way it made me feel obligated to care something about my uncle in return, but it was hard not ever knowing the man personally. And he was gone now, so I'd never get the chance.

After leaving the factory, I took my time walking back to Monkey Drool's; I needed to think, and besides, I was getting tired from all the wandering back and forth across di island. It hadn't seemed that large when I'd arrived, even smaller than Key West, but then I didn't often walk from coast to coast on Key West, either; usually it was more like meander twenty feet and stop at the next pub. I was going to go home in great bar hopping shape, a marathon walker on an island where you could literally crawl to your next libation destination.

I wondered for a while what Jimmy Buffett would do if he found himself in my situation here on di island, but found it unhelpful when I remembered he'd just come out with Margaritaville Rum and hardly needed this tiny island factory. And I thought about calling my old friend Marty back in Minnesota, for his advice again, but he always complained that I just did the opposite of whatever he said. And Chester? He was crazy. That left that guy Jack having to decide for himself once more.

It took some deep thought while shuffling along in my flip flops and leaning on fences watching the goats, but I managed to find the heart of the matter and discovered it was this; hell yes, I wanted a rum factory! What fun loving, beach going, boat drinking, pirate wannabee wouldn't want one? But I also wanted a parrot and a monkey and an iguana, too, but had absolutely no desire to take care of any of them. If I didn't want the responsibility of owning a lizard, how could I possibly handle the responsibility of an entire factory? It wouldn't be fair to myself or to di islanders to start this thing and then back out down the road when I got tired of dealing with it.

And I've never been much of a gambling man, either, and didn't want to bet my almost perfect life in the Keys against a new rum flavored one here on di island. There was plenty of rums to be found at the Rum Barrel Bar in Key West; about a hundred of them, in fact. Risking the good thing I already had for one that might be even better seemed almost like greed.

So shortly after turning east at the Crossroads towards Monkey Drool's I decided to just go back home, and store all the fine memories of this trip safely in my hold and be thankful for this wonderful adventure I'd had. I spent another hour walking at a snail's pace while chatting with myself and bumping up my confidence that my decision was the right one, just to make sure I wouldn't start waffling again, and by the time I finally arrived at the bar darkness had fallen over di island. I found Crazy Chester chatting amidst a large crowd of di islanders and he spotted me and waved, and came over to greet me, grinning happily.

"Jack! They told me all about the factory; congratulations!" he said. "You must be the luckiest guy on the planet; you're gonna be a rum tycoon! That's just groovy. Could there be anything better? I mean, I own a bar, but this, this is...this is...this is..."

"Great, yes, amazing, wonderful," I said, interrupting him before he started crying tears of joy for me. "Look, I need to talk to you."

"Okay," said Chester, and he followed me down to the beach.

As soon as we were far enough from the bar crowd to not be heard, I said, "When are you going home?"

Chester looked at me and blinked. "I just got here ten minutes ago," he said. "You want me to leave already?"

"No. Well, yes, but...not just you," I said. "I need a ride back to the Keys."

"Right this second?" said Chester. "My beer is still at the bar."

"No, not right this second! Just, whenever you were planning on going," I said.

Chester thought about it. "I was gonna go back on Sunday," he said. "But if you need to get back sooner I suppose I could leave tomorrow morning. Have you got some emergency rum business you need to take care of? And did I say how great I think the whole thing is?"

"Yes, several times," I said.

"I'll be glad to help you out whenever I can," said Chester. "Let me guess; right now you need to go pick up some bottles; or maybe some casks, or; I know! You need to go hire a Swedish bikini rum team!"

"No, I...a Swedish bikini rum team?" I said. "Never mind. I'm just going to say it. I'm not opening the factory and I want to get back home before di islanders kill me with machetes or kindness."

"You mean, you don't want to stay here and make rum on a tropical island?" said Chester.

"No, I don't," I said.

"And they call *me* crazy," said Chester. He looked up at the bar where di islanders were gathered. "Have you told them yet?" he asked.

"No," I said.

"Don't you think you should?" said Chester.

"Of course. I was just thinking it might be easier, not to mention safer, if I shouted it from the back of your boat about fifty feet off shore as we sailed away," I said.

Chester gave me a parental look, and I sighed.

"Oh, all right," I said. "I was just kidding, anyway. I'm not about to leave without telling them the truth; they've been too nice to me. Could you help me out, though? Get me started? It's not going to be easy."

"Sure. I'll do everything I can," he said. We walked back up to the bar, and Chester shouted, "Can I have your attention, please? Jack has some really bad news for you," and the crowd turned to face me.

"Thanks, Chester," I said evenly. "There's no easy way to say this. I have to leave tomorrow. And I won't be opening the rum factory."

My words were met with dead silence, which was worse than any of the reactions I'd been expecting, except for the screaming lynch mob.

"I wish someone would say something," I said.

"What do you want us to say?" said Ernesto. "Of course we want you to stay and run the factory."

"I know, but I just can't," I said.

"Yes, you just said that," said Ernesto.

"But why, boss?" said Faith.

"I guess it's mostly because I like the life I have in Key West," I said. "And I've only had it for about a year, so I hate to give it up already. Sure, there's a lot more hustle and bustle than there is here, and sometimes the tourists can be a pain in the ass. And yes, it would be nice if it was a bit more unspoiled like di island. But in a way it's the best of two worlds. It's like the mainland United States got busy with the Caribbean, and Key West was their love child. I can still do all the things I like to do, go to movies, watch football, grab a pizza, but with a tropical beat."

"We have pizza here," said Cavin.

"You do?" I said.

"Well, sometimes. When Gus flies us some in," said Cavin.

"Him again," I said. "Don't get me wrong, everyone; I do really like it here. And I like all you guys, and how great you've been to me since I got here. But I quit my job back in Minnesota to get away from the pressures of having a real job, and running a rum factory, as glamorous as it sounds, has to be at least as stressful as public relations."

"But you'd be di boss, boss," said Faith. "And you could just give di pressure to everyone else."

"True, but still...I just can't do it. I'd love to help you guys out but my mind is made up. I promise I won't stop until I have a buyer for the place that wants to reopen it as a rum factory; I swear," I said.

"I don't think anyone is going to want to start a business on this little island," said Ernesto. "And besides, we don't want someone else to run the factory. We want you, and your uncle Billy wanted you to have it, too."

They weren't making this easy, that was for sure. I wanted someone to get angry and argumentative; hell, I'd have settled for some good old Brittany style snippiness. It was a very effective debate technique, this love in they were hitting me with. But I held my ground, shakier than a volcanic island though it was.

"But Billy didn't know me, and I didn't know him," I said. "I can't trade my slightly crazy life in the Keys for an even crazier one here just because my nutty uncle wanted me to. I'm not Luke Skywalker and he wasn't Obi-Wan Kenobi, and I'm not becoming a Jedi to follow him on some damned fool idealistic crusade."

"Who is Obi-Wan Kenobi?" asked Faith.

"I tink he used to own da fish gutters, didn't he?" asked the Innkeeper.

"No, that was John Bawani," said Roger.

"Ah, dat's right," said the Innkeeper. "Den who is-"

"Never mind!" I said, reminding myself to steer clear of cultural references when talking to di islanders. "The point is...well, I forgot what my point is. Now I remember. The point is, I like it here, I like all of you, but my decision is final; I'm going home tomorrow."

"And they call *me* crazy," said Chester.

"Would you stop saying that?" I said.

There was another long silence, then Ernesto said, "We understand. Di island isn't for everyone. And we hope you are happy and come back and visit us one day. You are a good man."

I didn't feel like a good man; I felt more like the evil emperor. "Thank you," I said. "And I will visit some time, I promise. But now I think I want some time by myself. If I could just get a bottle of rum..."

That may not have been the most tactful thing to ask for, but it was what I needed. The Innkeeper took a bottle of Cruzan from behind the bar and passed it to me, and I gave him some money and walked down to the sea. I found a chair I liked and sat down to drown my feelings in the stuff I wouldn't be making.

I never would have dreamed it would be possible to feel sad about going *to* the Keys. I guess it was a case of wanting to have your Key Lime pie and rum, too. I considered briefly the notion of living on di island *and* Key West, but it didn't seem practical. I wasn't that rich, and it would probably be years before the factory wouldn't need my supervision, and I couldn't be in two places at once; unless maybe I changed my mind and got that Jedi training from Yoda.

In a way I wished the whole thing had never happened, because I couldn't shake the feeling that no matter what I did now it was going to lead to pangs of regret. But that was life; sometimes you came to a fork in the road and you had to try not to agonize over what would have happened if you had taken one of the other tines instead.

I sat watching the ocean tease the sand for a while in a daze, until I caught a whiff of coconut and perfume. I was about to look to see where the heavenly smell was coming from, when a tall, curvy figure stomped into view a few feet in front of me.

"Ees it true?" said Isabella sharply, her eyes flashing angrily but beautifully at me.

"Um," I said, overwhelmed by suddenly having this living and even more lovely version of my Maria in such close proximity to my person, and talking to me. Even if she looked ready to belt me.

"Well? They said joo are leaving? And that joo are not opening the factory?" she demanded.

"It's complicated, and I really wish I could help, but...yes. I'm afraid it's true," I said, somewhat meekly.

Isabella let loose with a tirade of Spanish that would have made an alligator cringe and hide under the bed. I wasn't sure if there were any expletives involved, but it sounded like nothing but. Then she leaned down and put one hand on each arm of my chair and got face to face with me.

"Then let me tell joo something, meester big shot American," she said, as I tried to look her in her brown eyes and not at all her brown skin that was threatening to spill out of her turquoise top. "They were going to throw joo a party tomorrow night. They wanted to thank joo for coming here and giving them a better place to work. Did joo know that many of the people who came and worked for joo lost their jobs in the sugar cane fields?"

"They did?" I said. Just what I needed; more guilt.

"Jes! Rodrigo fired them all. Now they will have to go beg for their jobs back, and he will hire them but at even less pay than before," said Isabella.

"I didn't know that," I said.

"Of course not! Joo didn't bother to find out," she said, standing up and causing the coffee colored hills of Columbia to rise past my very eyes. "But they will survive, because they are strong. So go home to America. We don't need joo. They don't need joo," she said, then she stomped off down the beach.

My first meeting with Isabella hadn't gone at all like I'd imagined it would so many times after first seeing her, although I did get almost as physically close as I had in some of my more vivid daydreams. I watched her go until she was out of sight, thinking it might be the last time I'd ever see her, and I wondered if my Maria would mind if I changed her name to Isabella.

"Now and then we hoped that if we lived and were good, God would permit us to be pirates." -Mark Twain

Chapter 10

I wandered along the the water's edge in the opposite direction from Isabella's departure, rum bottle in hand. It seemed quieter than usual, and I realized it was because there was no music or sounds of laughter coming from Monkey Drool's; I'd evidently squashed that. I came again to the old fishing boat and found the ghost of Captain Black Dog in the back half of the vessel, seated in one of the chairs by her aft railing.

"Be ye friend or foe?" he said.

"Well, I'm not a foe so I guess that leaves me a friend," I said. "You're Captain Black Dog, aren't you?"

"How do you know my name?" he asked suspiciously.

I thought for a moment. "Jolly Roger told me," I said.

"Ah. Good man, and a fine pirate be he," said Black Dog. "What's that ye be carrying?"

I held up the bottle. "It's rum," I said. "I'd be willing to share it."

"Hm. Ya look harmless enough, I be thinkin'," said Black Dog. "Climb aboard, then, matey! A man with rum is a friend indeed."

I hoisted myself up onto the boat and into the seat next to my new pirate friend and held out the bottle. He took it, proving he either wasn't a ghost or that Hollywood had it wrong all these years.

Black Dog took a long swig, then wiped his mouth with the back of his puffy sleeve, and handed the bottle back to me. "Thanks, lad. That be most welcome on a still and portentous night."

"It is quiet, isn't it?" I said.

"Aye; too quiet. Something be wrong on this eve," said Black Dog.

He might be crazy, this pirate, but he had keen senses.

I took a drink from my bottle and thought about telling him what was going on, but it would be a long story and I didn't know if a ghost pirate would care. Then again he might care too much, and decide to run me through for cutting off the rum again. Instead I decided to ask for his advice, as if that made some sort of sense.

"Let me ask you something, Captain," I said. "Let's say a pirate had a decent sized treasure chest at his home port, you know the kind, filled with swag that made him happy. And there was this other treasure chest, even bigger, on a far away island, possibly guarded with pitfalls and traps galore. The legends say there might be a great treasure inside, but no one knows for sure, so even if he were to manage to dig it up it might come to nothing."

"I'm with ye so far, laddie," said Black Dog.

I handed him the rum bottle back and continued. "My question is, should he stay in his home port and enjoy spending the treasure he already has, or should he leave, perhaps for years, to go on a quest for the unknown treasure with no guarantee of success."

"Is the first treasure safely buried? Will it still be there when he returns?" said Black Dog.

"It should be, yes. *If* he ever manages to return. And he would lose all the time he could have spent enjoying his first treasure," I said. "Plus, it might be really stressful, er, dangerous, to go after the bigger treasure; he might not ever be the same afterwards."

"I see what ye be sayin', lad," said Black Dog. "But every pirate be different and has to follow their own instincts, or they be doomed. Now if it were me, for instance...well, if there be bigger treasure on the horizon then I'll be goin' after it; let the landlubbers stay warm and safe at home in their beds. It's adventure I'll always be seekin' as long as long as I can draw a breath." He took another guzzle from the rum bottle and handed it back.

He made a good pirate, this Black Dog, I'll give him that, and he made a convincing argument to boot. I was still going back to Key West, of course; my mind was made up, and no ghost was going to change that, no matter how many Sparrow and Barbosa like chestnuts he threw my way. But at least now I felt like a jerk *and* a coward, so things were moving right along.

I took one more drink from the bottle and gave it to Black Dog. "Keep it. I've had enough of rum for a while, I guess," I said.

"Thank ye, matey! Ye be a fine lad," said Black Dog.

"Smooth sailing to you, Captain," I said.

I climbed off the boat and was walking away when Black Dog shouted at me. "Hold up there, a minute; here," he said, and tossed me a small object.

I tried to catch it, but it was dark, and it fell into the sand. I got down on my hands and knees to search for it, and found a small, circular metal item about the size of a quarter. I stood up and blew the sand off it and examined it, holding it up in the moonlight.

It was a small, rusted metal compass, the kind of thing they used to put in Cracker Jack boxes as a prize before everything turned plastic. It looked old and worn, but it still seemed to work, or at least it spun around as I moved it.

"Thanks," I said. "Is it magic? Will it point towards whatever I want the most?"

"It won't guide ye to what you want the most," said Black Dog. "Only you can know where that lies. But it is magic."

"How so?" I said.

"You see all those markings around the outer rim?" said Black Dog.

I looked closely, but could barely make them out. "Yes, I see them."

"Those all be directions you can go from where ye be standin'; with that compass in your hand the whole horizon is yours to sail," said Black Dog. "Or you can plant yer flag right in the center where ye already be. The choice is yours, laddie."

I looked at the compass, then nodded and gripped it tightly in my hand. "Thank you, Captain. I'll keep it with me always."

"Farewell, matey," said Black Dog, and I turned and walked off into the night, feeling more uncertain of myself than ever.

"The average man will bristle if you say his father was dishonest, but he will brag a little if he discovers his great grandfather was a pirate." -Bern Williams

Chapter 11

Many of di islanders were gathered by the docks the next day when I came down to meet up with Chester. Cavin had picked me up in the jeep again; he didn't say anything about the factory and just small talked about my trip home. Di islanders didn't say much either as I made my way through the crowd, just a few muttered goodbyes and well wishes. Most of the people I knew best on di island were there; Roger, Faith, Ernesto, Luis, the Innkeeper, Jedidiah, Boyd...and Isabella, standing off by herself, arms crossed and looking drop dead beautiful, in more ways than one.

I walked out onto the unsteady dock to the Lazy Lizard, which was tied up where Gus' plane had been a few days before. Chester was busy getting ready for departure while keeping a wary eye on a flock of seagulls that were circling overhead. I dropped my bags over the boat railing and took one last look around me.

Di islanders were all turned towards me up on shore, looking glum. I considered taking their picture, gathered together like they were, but it didn't seem right, as if I didn't deserve it. And anyway, I preferred the stored memories I already had of any one of our nights at Monkey Drool's, di islanders smiling happily, over some digital copy of a moment that looked like it belonged at someone's funeral.

Chester stood watching me, finished with his preparations, then said, "Are you sure you want to do this?"

"Positive," I said. "I just think it's the right thing to do."

"Got to be the most depressed looking people in one place I've ever seen for someone doing the right thing," said Chester, shaking his head.

I climbed on board the Lizard, and Chester went to the back of the boat and leaned way out to untie the aft line as I prepared to say goodbye to di island.

Suddenly Jolly Roger came running down the dock, causing it to sway madly about, which in turn caused the aft line to jerk the boat, which in turn caused Chester to utter, "Dang it!" just before he hit the water with a splash.

"Jack, wait," said Roger.

"Look, I have to go," I said, trying to decide if Chester needed rescuing or not.

"Yes, I know you do, but there's something I tink you should know before you go; something we should have told you from di start," said Roger.

"What is it?" I said impatiently.

"You know di ghost? Captain Black Dog?" said Roger.

"I know of an old guy in a pirate outfit," I said. "Whether or not he's a ghost is still open for debate."

"Yes, but what you don't know and should know is who he really is," said Roger. "Jack, di ghost is your uncle, Billy."

"Come again?" I said.

"It's true; Captain Black Dog be your uncle," said Roger.

"Why the hell didn't somebody tell me?" I snapped. "What is it with everyone from my family to you keeping Billy a secret?"

"Dat's part of the reason, right there," said Roger. "We thought with di way your family felt about him it would better not to tell you; we didn't know if you would feel di same way about Billy as they did."

I sighed. "I guess I can see that; it still makes me mad, though. All my life I've had this uncle who's far more interesting than anyone else in my family, and I never even knew he existed. And now I almost left di island not knowing he was here and alive, and that I'd just met and talked with him."

"I know, mon; I'm sorry," said Roger.

"Don't apologize; at least you told me in time," I said. "So what happened to Billy, anyway? Why is he the way he is?"

"It happened when his boat sank. He was sailing back from Key West and a storm suddenly came up. Billy was a good sailor, but the winds blew him off course, and he hit a reef. Di boat broke in half and Billy dived into di water and managed to swim to shore."

"Wait, so is that his boat down the beach from Monkey Drool's?" I asked.

"Yes, and it's di one he talks about sinking, too," said Roger.

"And that made him go insane? It was just a boat," I said.

"Well, Billy was always a little unstable to begin with. But di boat was also di only way he had to make money to open di factory, and he wanted it so bad," said Roger. "But what I tink may have hurt him the most was his dog."

"His dog; the collar in the office...Sammy, right?" I said.

"Aye. Sammy be a big Black Lab mutt, and he be Billy's best friend for years, traveling everywhere with him. Sammy was on board when di boat sank. Billy searched and searched di island hoping to find Sammy alive, but he found him washed up on shore; he be di one buried in di cemetery. After dat Billy went into his own little world."

"Captain Black Dog," I said.

"Ya, mon. Billy Danielson truly died di night of the storm," said Roger.

"And became a ghost," I said.

"We just humor him now," said Roger. "We say, if Billy wants to be a pirate ghost, then so be it."

"And the will? Was that a fake too, then?" I said.

"No, di will be real; your uncle wanted you to have di factory. We figured if Billy thought he was dead then that be close enough for us. And we thought if you came and got di factory up and running it might ease some of his pain," said Roger.

"Unreal," I said. "You know, it would have been nice if everyone would have just come out and told me all this before."

"Would it have made a difference?" said Roger.

"Hell, yeah!" I said, trying to figure out exactly how. The only thing I could come up with at first was that now my uncle wasn't dead. But then there was this matter of all the people, especially my family, and most especially my grandfather, Darth Vader, who had spent all those years keeping Billy out of my life. That pissed me off, and the last time I got pissed off I sold everything I owned and took off to be happy. If trying to open the factory was as stupid a thing to do as it sounded, then that was exactly what I wanted to do now, partially because I knew it would drive my father crazy; revenge was a dish best served with rum.

I literally jumped at the idea, over the boat railing and onto the dock, making it swing sharply to one side.

"Dang it!" said Chester, falling once more into the water he had just managed to climb back out of.

"Sorry, Chester!" I said. "Roger, could you give him a hand?"

Roger went over to do so and I hurried my way to shore.

Di islanders gathered around me, probably wondering what was up. I couldn't help feeling kind of stupid all of a sudden; I had this big thing to say and I had no idea how to say it without sounding like a pompous ass, as in *"Here I am to save the day!"* like some kind of rum superhero.

"Okay," I said finally. "I don't know how I can say this without it sounding like a proclamation. Oh, the hell with it; it *is* a proclamation. I, Jack Danielson, am going to stay and try to open the rum factory."

Di islanders stood quietly staring at me; not the sort of reaction I'd been expecting, which was something closer to a ticker-tape parade.

"Do you mean it, senor?" asked Ernesto. "Truly?"

"Yes. I'm going to do my best," I said.

"Let's hear it for di boss!" Faith shouted, and a nicely festive outpouring of cheers and thank yous followed.

Isabella stood nearby, watching intently, a bemused look on her face; "The hell with it!" I said, and I grabbed her and pulled her into my arms and kissed her passionately.

Okay, that last bit didn't happen, except for the part where she stood watching intently, a bemused look on her face. But I did think about doing it.

"Will we be able to start on Monday, senor?" asked Ernesto.

"Ya, mon, we should get right to work," said Jedidiah.

"Whoa, hold on," I said. "I don't see how that's going to be possible. There's really nothing we can do until I sit down with Luis, and...where is Luis?"

"Right here, Jack," he said, holding up his hand from the back row.

"We have to get together and figure out what we should do first to get this thing started," I said.

"I'll go to the factory and make a list of what we need to order," said Luis.

"Good. After we get all the basics shipped in *then* we can start talking about jobs and officially getting the place open," I said.

"But that could take weeks," said Ernesto. "And many of us don't have jobs anymore because of Rodrigo."

There was a murmuring of agreement from the crowd.

"If there was anything I could do to help now, I would, but this is going to take time," I said.

"Di place could use a fresh coat of paint, boss," said Faith.

"That's probably true," I said. "But-"

"And di floor still needs repairing, along with di walls and di plumbing," said Faith.

"Maybe, but-" I said.

"And di wiring and di trucks and di lights need to be fixed, too," said Faith.

I needed to stop her while I was behind. She was right, though; the factory was in nowhere near the condition it needed to be to make rum. Unfortunately my old PR job had given me no clues as to how to actually get anything done. That had been my boss, Mr. Strickland's job; mine had been to do whatever he said. But then I realized all I had to do was the same thing he had done, minus all the yelling and bitching, which mostly was to delegate authority.

"You're right, Faith," I said. "And since you have a much better idea of what the factory needs than I do, I'm making you its supervisor."

"Me? But I thought Luis would be in charge,"said Faith. "I don't know how to make di rum."

"Luis will be in charge of the rum; your job will be to hire and supervise the workers. And you can start by hiring people to take care of everything you just mentioned to me. If that's alright with you, Luis," I said.

"Sure; Faith is probably the most sensible person on di island," said Luis.

"Then it's settled, if you'll take the job, Faith," I said.

Faith considered things. "Does dat mean I'd be his boss, too?" she said, pointing at Ernesto.

"If you decide to hire him, yes," I said.

"Den I accept!" said Faith happily.

"Aye, carumba," groaned Ernesto.

"Now you have to do everyting I say," Faith said.

"So nothing has changed," said Ernesto.

"Nope," said Faith.

"So where can I find this Rodrigo and his sugar plantation?" I said.

"Are you gonna go talk to him?" said Jedidiah.

"Yes. We're going to need his sugar, which will benefit him, too. I'll see if I can get him to be more reasonable about things," I said.

"Good luck with dat," said Faith. "Dey say Rodrigo is part jackass, and dat's di good part. Just go up di north road; you can't miss di plantation."

This Rodrigo might be part mule, but he hadn't met the new Jack Danielson yet. I was a rum tycoon now, and more. Luke Skywalker's uncle Owen had died and it made him want to become a Jedi. My uncle Billy might still be alive but I was going to become one, too.

I hoped it would make my grandpa Vader spin in his grave.

"Rum has been called by many other names, including Nelson's Blood and Kill-Devil."

Chapter 12

The sugar plantation was up in the northeast corner of di island. It was Sunday, which I figured was why there were no workers present, but I couldn't find Rodrigo at first, either. As I wandered around looking for him I couldn't help noticing how lousy the place looked. I knew nothing about growing sugar cane, but to me the plants I saw didn't look healthy, and the plantation itself seemed to be falling apart. The fences and buildings were in worse condition than our factory, and the equipment looked rusty and old.

I finally found who I assumed to be Rodrigo sitting on the porch of his house, which was in as bad a shape as the rest of the property. And Rodrigo himself was a mess as well; short, overweight, his belly protruding from under a stained tank top, his long, unkempt hair sticking out like a disused parrot's nest. He watched me approach as he drank a cerveza and munched on an unidentified chicken part.

"Are you Rodrigo?" I asked.

He belched at me, then said, "Si. Who are you?"

"I'm Jack Danielson. I'm the new owner of the rum factory," I said.

"I heard you were leaving," said Rodrigo. News did indeed travel fast on di island.

"I changed my mind," I said.

"Then you must be crazy, gringo, to want to stay here," he said. Seems like I couldn't win; crazy if I did, crazy if I didn't. "What do you want, anyway?"

"I came to talk to you about your plantation and di islanders. Some of them want to come back to work for you, but they're afraid you're going to pay them next to nothing," I said.

"Maybe they're not so stupid after all," said Rodrigo.

"So it's true? You are going to blackmail them?" I said, feeling like some labor union leader in a movie. "You know, when we get the factory running we're going to need sugar. It would be best to get it from you, right here on di island. It would be good for you, and good for me. But you need to treat the workers fairly if we're going to buy from you."

Rodrigo stood up, all five foot nothing of him. "Are you trying to tell me how to run my plantation, senor?" he said gruffly.

"No, just asking you to take your workers back at the same pay they left at," I said.

"I can't do that," Rodrigo said.

"Why not?" I said.

"Because the plantation is closed," said Rodrigo.

"Closed?" I said. "None of di islanders mentioned the plantation being closed. Since when?"

"Since you started needing my sugar cane," said Rodrigo.

"That doesn't make any sense," I said. "You could be making good money for a change."

"Or I could be sitting in an air conditioned office," said Rodrigo.

"Meaning?" I said.

"My brother Phillippe just bought a Best Western in Boise, and he wants me to come in as a partner," said Rodrigo.

"Sounds like a dream come true," I said.

"It is; I want to get out of this business and go to America and be a rich merchant, wear a suit, drive a big car, and have a skinny blonde girlfriend," said Rodrigo dreamily.

"Good luck with that," I said. "But I still don't see what that has to do with me."

"I don't want the sugar. You need the sugar. There it is," said Rodrigo, pointing at a nearby field. "Twenty thousand American dollars and it's yours."

"What? I don't have that kind of money to spare. If I gave you that much cash I wouldn't have enough left to finish opening the factory and pay the workers," I said.

Rodrigo shrugged. "All I know is it's going to be difficult to make rum without sugar cane."

"Why you little..." I said. This was just the sort of thing I'd been trying to avoid when I set out to live my life like...never mind. I'd officially owned the factory for about an hour now and already I was trying to negotiate labor disputes and solve supply problems. "I'm going to have to get back to you."

"Take your time, gringo; but not too much time. America, she waits for me, and the sugar harvest will come soon. Or it would if there was anyone working here to wield the cane knives," said Rodrigo calmly.

America can have him, I thought to myself. He'll get eaten alive by the fast paced lifestyle of Boise.

I left the plantation and made my way back south. I wasn't sure what to call this current song I was living, the *"Rodrigo is blackmailing me with his sugar cane"* tune. It wasn't very catchy and I didn't like my co-writer much. The last time I'd been in anything close to such a dire situation was back at the Schooner Wharf Bar in Key West when they'd run out of Kalik beer one sunny afternoon; it was pretty tense for a few seconds, but I avoided any costly psychotherapy by switching to Landsharks for the rest of the day.

But this sugar thing was an even bigger problem. One of the pluses I'd seen to opening the factory during my inner debate sessions was the fact that sugar was grown right here on di island. If I ended up having to import it it was bound to lower my profit margin. Profit margin; those were two ugly back to back words. I preferred pairings like sandy beach, Pina Colada and Conch Fritters. But it occurred to me that running di rum factory, stressful as it might occasionally be, would be like bartending on a giant scale. My rum could aid thousands in a noble cause, to help other people live their lives like a Jimmy Buffett song. Maybe a little worry was worth that after all.

It wasn't as if I was totally destitute; I did have some ill gotten booty stashed away, otherwise I wouldn't be attempting this to begin with. I'd blown a pretty large yolk of that public relations earned nest egg traveling and having a good time, while trying to work out who the hell Jack Danielson was so I could start being him instead of this other guy. After that my bank account had stayed more or less at the same level over the next year while I bartended in Key West, except for when my condo in Minneapolis finally sold, pushing my funds back into a more temperate latitude.

So I did still have some thousands of dollars available to me, since it turned out that ten years of hard work, saving, and investing takes longer to blow on a good time than I would have thought. But if I was forced to hand Rodrigo twenty grand it would put a ding in my funds as large as the Peterbilt had put in my

Suburban, and I would very possibly end up like Billy, broke and wandering di island. I wasn't sure if it was big enough for two pirate ghosts.

I thought about trying a Mexican standoff with Rodrigo, but he was Latin and would have a huge advantage coming out of the gate. And during that time no one would be able to work in the fields, and the factory couldn't open because of no sugar, so there'd be no jobs for anyone anywhere. I didn't want to be the cause of mass unemployment; I wasn't English Petroleum.

I'd figure it out all somehow, though. I had to. I was committed to a course of action for the second time in as many years, and it was fast becoming an annual event. Some people made New Years resolutions; mine just kept popping up whenever the hell they felt like it with no regard to any calendar I could perceive. Hopefully my latest decree would fit right inside the first.

Jack and di rum song.

Sounded pretty damned Buffettish to me.

"During fermentation, yeast and water are added to the molasses or sugarcane juice in large tanks, and the yeast converts the sugar into alcohol."

Chapter 13

A week later the factory condition continued to improve and Rodrigo continued to hold the sugar hostage. I didn't see any signs he was about to cave, and many of di islanders seemed to be getting worried, at least as worried as islanders get. There were enough odd jobs around the factory to keep many of the people occupied for the time being, and Faith kept coming up with more. But sooner or later we'd run out of things for everyone to do until we opened, and without sugar I wasn't sure when that would be.

And we hit yet another snag when Faith tried to order some new light fixtures. They were too big for Gus to fly in and I couldn't really ask Crazy Chester, who had just arrived back home to his own business in the Keys, to pick them up and bring them to us. The problem was with di island dock system; the ones where I had arrived were so old, small, and rickety that boats of any real size, captained by sane skippers anyway, refused to come in. And while there were some larger concrete docks near the small power plant in the northeast corner of di island, they were badly damaged as well and unsafe to use.

So I had no choice but to have them all repaired; they all needed it and it would be good for di island (and it might keep Crazy Chester out of the drink for a few more seconds) but it meant more expenses again. What we really could have used was a small airport, but that wasn't going to happen unless Jimmy himself showed up and offered to pay for one, and since he seemed to prefer to land in the water anyway it wasn't likely to happen anytime soon.

But life continued on and another Friday night rolled around, and once again there was to be a big shindig on the beach. This time di islanders said they had a surprise for me; an initiation of sorts. I made them promise it wouldn't involve goats, piercings in odd places, or Jaegermeister, and steeled myself for whatever was to come.

There was a large crowd of di islanders at Monkey Drool's when I arrived, but Roger intercepted me before I could join them and took me aside. "This isn't going to maim any of my body parts, is it?" I said. "Because for some reason I'm fairly happy with my appearance and not really in the market right now for any grizzly scars to add to it."

"About the only thing it might maim is your liver," said Roger with a grin.

"Ah, well, it's used to being kicked around by now so maim away," I said. "What is this all about, then, anyway?"

"Tonight you become an islander," said Roger.

"I do?" I said.

"Yes. You become a part of us and we become a part of you," said Roger.

That sounded harmless enough, but then so had biting into my first Habanero Pepper. I'd almost called the fire department on that one, and I wasn't sure who to alert on di island if some part of me suddenly burst into flames tonight. "I'm honored," I said. "What do I do?"

"Come with me," said Roger.

He led me a ways down the beach until we came to a big wooden chair sitting in the middle of nowhere, with a smaller chair facing it and two tiki torches lighting the area. The chair looked like a medieval throne, high backed with large armrests. On one side of it sat a table, and on the other an open wooden chest. "Dis be di island," said Roger, pointing at the chest. "All these tings be di people who live here."

"What do you mean?" I asked.

Roger dug around in the chest for a moment. "Dis be me," he said, holding up a yellow smiley face button, then he dug some more. "And dis peace sign be your uncle Billy. And dis blown out flip flop be Crazy Chester, from the day he stopped wearing shoes."

"So every object in the chest represents someone on di island?" I said.

"Or someone who once lived or spent a lot of time here, like Chester," said Roger. "Dey be talismans of a sort. Dis gonna be you, laddie," he said, holding up an airline bottle of Captain Morgan, a relative of my empty old friends from the Ramada Inn who had helped in my escape from the ordinary. "You be di rum."

"Perfect," I said, then leaned down to examine the chest and its contents more closely. "This is really something. So what do I do to get my bottle in there?"

"First, sit in di throne," said Roger.

I did so, and felt rather kingly. "Now what?"

"Now di islanders will come to you, one by one. Dey will bring you a small gift and put it on di table, then sit down across from you and tell you something about themselves that you didn't know. And you must tell them something, too. Whatever you like, a big secret or a little one; it doesn't matter," explained Roger. "That way you know us and we know you better."

I immediately started thinking about what to say; I'd never done anything remotely like this before, and I wasn't sure at first if I had anything worth confiding to anyone. But the more I thought about it the more I realized we all have little quirks and secrets that nobody knows about, and I had my share, too, although I wasn't sure anyone would be all that interested in my insistence in using exactly eight squares of toilet paper.

Roger left me to join the others, and soon after Boyd came and put a bottle of Red Stripe on the table and sat down. I was surprised that he'd been the first since we hadn't really talked that much since my arrival, but I supposed they probably didn't have a batting order, either.

"I'll start," said Boyd, brushing his long hair out of his face. "I've never touched any kind of drugs or alcohol in my life," he said.

So much for stereotypes, I thought to myself; bongos, long hair, and an almost comatose laid back personality. I would have sworn;.but when I thought about it, I couldn't remember seeing him with an alcoholic drink in his hand at Monkey's. But it was time for my confession. "I have; drugs, I mean," I said. "When a pretty girl at a party asks you if you want to get high, what can you do? And I didn't even get to first base for all my lawlessness."

Boyd smiled and stood up, and said "Welcome to di island, man," and went back to Monkey Drool's.

I picked up my Red Stripe and took a drink, and the Innkeeper came next. He gave me a coconut mug of his Pickled Parrot Punch and sat down. "My real name is Franny," he said.

The secrets were getting big already; that had been a bold one. One bombshell deserved another, so I braced myself and said, "I drank Zima for one summer," and utterly failed to feel better after getting it off my conscience. The Innkeeper welcomed me and left for the bar. I already had two beverages beside me; I was going to have to either speed up my drinking or drag out my confessions.

Thankfully Ernesto brought me a plate with a couple of delicious crab cakes, and an admission that when he lived in Mexico he had illegally sneaked into the United States, but snuck back out because he didn't like California very much. I told him the story about how I woke up in bed next to a man in New Orleans during Mardi Gras, which gave him a good laugh.

Islanders came and went as the night went on; Cavin used to be in a little known boy band in Cali, Luis had almost quit the rum business when he got an offer from a vacationing tourist who worked at the Jack Daniels factory (a weird little coinky-dink for me), Faith had posed semi-nude for a magazine in the Bahamas, something even Ernesto didn't know, and Roger had taken anti-depressant pills for a while until he realized that taking the pills was what was depressing him. Other islanders passed on similar stories, all in all nothing Earth shattering. In return I told them my New Orleans story a few more times, my Jaegermeister and Wendy old college try and fail to get the girl tale, and confessed that no matter how hard I tried, wanted, and felt I should like raw oysters, I just couldn't do it.

As time went on and the food, drink, and trinkets piled up next to me, my tongue became looser and my secrets a little more open and embarrassing, such as why I'd switched from briefs to boxers. Maybe that was the point, especially with alcohol involved; there was a certain wisdom to it. I didn't personally have anything big to get off my chest (other than the Zima), but if I had I met have let it slip out and lightened my load for it. Even so, it still made me feel good, and closer to di islanders, telling them these little tidbits. And I stand by my decision after seeing the look on Wonbago's face to not repeat my boxers and briefs story.

And then suddenly she was in the chair across from me, looking as radiant as always. She sat staring through me again, and it felt as though I didn't have any secrets left to tell her that she couldn't already see.

"I think I may have misjudged you," Isabella said at last, evidently done reading my mind. "Maybe joo are not such a bad man after all."

I sat looking back at her, wondering if that was her secret. It wasn't the passionate confession of undying lust and love I'd been hoping for, but it was a baby step in the right direction; at least she didn't seem to hate me anymore.

"I like you," my tongue said suddenly and completely without permission, and I vowed to give it a good tongue lashing later. I hadn't wanted to say that; it wasn't my style. My style was to wait a length of time proportionate to how unobtainable I felt the woman in question was before I made any sort of move, and in Isabella's case that would have been about ten years. But it seemed my tongue could no longer tell time; must've been the rum.

"I know," said Isabella, looking away. "All the men do."

"But I really like you," my tongue continued. All sorts of orders were being shouted in my head, and mass confusion reigned on deck as I tried in vain to get my words under control, but to no avail; the chain of command had completely broken down.

"Ees that joor secret?" said Isabella.

"Was that yours?" I said.

"No," said Isabella. "I was going to tell joo that I love American football."

"You do?" I said.

"Jes. My cousin in Miami took me to a Dolphin's game once, and eet was the best thing ever," said Isabella.

"Will you marry me?" I thought.

"And Aaron Rodgers, he ees so dreamy," Isabella continued.

"Maybe not," I thought. Mixed marriages could sometimes work, but Vikings-Packers?

"What were joo going to tell me?" she asked.

"I think what I told you is what I really wanted to say," I said, contrary to all the disciplinary measures I was considering for my speech center.

Isabella stood up. "I didn't bring joo a gift," she said. "So here." And with that she leaned down and lightly kissed me on the lips, then turned and walked away.

My tongue sat back and gloated, insufferably pleased with himself; there'd be no living with him now. Although my lips pointed out that he hadn't been involved in the kiss, so maybe he wasn't all that after all.

Whatever or whoever had been responsible for Isabella's gift, it had beat the hell out of the Innkeeper's punch, especially if it was the thought that counted. I felt like telling each of di islanders that would follow the same secret; Isabella Vaccaria had kissed me. But I managed to hold my tongue, if a bit belatedly.

Not all di islanders came by, which was just as well since my table runneth over with goodies as it was. Rodrigo for one was absent, which also was just as well unless he wanted to let slip how long this lockout of his was going to last. But I did share stories and secrets with roughly forty of di islanders, and when it was finished and they all came back down together and gathered around me, and Roger dropped my little bottle of rum in the chest and closed and locked it tight, I felt like I truly belonged on di island.

"Where we find rum, we find action, sometimes cruel, sometimes heroic, sometimes humorous, but always vigorous and interesting." -Charles Taussig

Chapter 14

The day had started out so well.

I'd gone by the factory as usual to see what kind of progress was being made, and if there was anything my pocketbook could help with. Faith told me we needed a few small things and I told her to put them on my new 3rd Bank of di island card. Nothing much else was going on, except that Luis had come to an arrangement with Cavin to make him his apprentice. Which was great; we needed someone young to learn the trade and take over in the future, and Cavin was a good, hard working, smart kid. In fact, he was good and hard working when I arrived, inside one of the stills, cleaning, polishing, and sanitizing, and being generally apprenticized.

When lunch rolled around Faith invited me to eat with she and Ernesto at their home, and we had a truly delectable meal of conch sandwiches and mangoes. I was feeling especially excellent as we walked down the dirt road towards the Crossroads, when Jedidiah, Boyd, and three of my workers came jogging up behind us, cheering and slapping each other on the back.

"What's going on?" I asked, anxious to add to my already good mood. "You guys look happy."

"We be great!" said Jedidiah. "And we got good news, boss."

"What is it?" I said anxiously.

"We just solved all di problems with Rodrigo," said Jedidiah.

"How?" I said. "Did you go talk to him?" I wondered how they might have made more of a convincing argument than I had, but then again, talking to Jedidiah would have been a helluva lot more intimidating than talking to me, being as large as an NFL linebacker and all that.

"Better," said Boyd, grinning ear to ear. "We set his sugar cane fields on fire. He'll have no choice but to sell the place to you now, cheap."

"You what? Are you crazy?" I said. "Wait a minute; I thought Ernesto told me that was one of the things you did to harvest the sugar cane, set it on fire. To kill the snakes and burn the dry leaves."

"Not when you do it like we did, and when," said Boyd.

"You can't just go around burning people's property like that," I said. "It's not right." I looked to the northeast and could see plumes of dark smoke rising up into the blue sky.

"And it was right for Rodrigo to fire everyone and to try and blackmail you into buying his plantation?" asked Jedidiah.

"Well, no, I suppose it wasn't, but-" I began.

"Irie, irie! Di workers have struck back at di man!" said Jedidiah, thrusting a coconut sized fist into the air.

I suppose in a way they were right; Rodrigo probably had it coming. But I was from America where striking back at the man was a lengthy and drawn out process involving lawyers in suits, and the man usually came out on top. This sort of thing would land your ass in jail in a big hurry, right or wrong. I just wasn't used to it being as simple as it was here.

"I understand why you did what you did," I said. "But what about the fields? We needed the cane for the rum and now it's all going to have to be regrown."

"You didn't want his sugar anyway, boss," said Ernesto.

"I didn't?" I said.

"No," said Ernesto. "Rodrigo knows nothing about growing good sugar cane."

"Okay; you know better than I do, although I wish someone would have mentioned that before. I would have been looking for an alternative," I said.

"We thought you wanted to buy the plantation and replant," said Ernesto. "All you talked about was using di island sugar."

"Actually what I talked about was using di island sugar but having Rodrigo grow it; just because he wanted to sell the place to me doesn't mean I wanted to buy it, but no matter," I said. "Just do me a favor, everyone. If you ever have a problem with myself or your job at the factory come and talk to me and we'll work it out, I promise; no fires, and no striking back at me the man, okay?"

"Okay, boss," said Jedidiah, smiling, and he shook my hand with a mitt that could have picked me up by my head.

"You all better get going before Rodrigo comes looking for you; hopefully he'll think it was just an accident," I said.

"Three fires in three different locations? I don't think so," said Boyd.

"Very thorough," I said. "But you better git, anyway."

The fire brigade moved on quickly down the road, as did Ernesto, Faith, and I. When we came to the Crossroads we split up, they heading back to the factory and work, and I to the east with the intention of snooping around the northeastern corner of di island. I'd been trying to find Captain Black Dog Billy for some time now with no luck; I wanted to see if I could make some sort of a connection with the uncle part of him. Roger told me he often disappeared for days without any ghostly sightings, so like any good pirate he probably had a hideout somewhere; perhaps there was a skull shaped cave on di island.

I was about to explore a small northern path going off the main easterly one when I heard a small engine sputtering down the road from the west. I turned to see an old motorcycle with a sidecar coming towards me, and it skidded to a halt nearby. The short, pudgy rider dismounted and took off his helmet, revealing Rodrigo's stubbled, angry looking mug.

I didn't know and didn't care if he'd been looking for me or how he found me, or if I'd just gotten lucky and been the first person he felt he could blame that he'd come across. What I cared about, and rather deeply, was the shotgun he grabbed out of the sidecar and quickly, and unfortunately quite deftly, pointed at me.

"Now hold on, Rodrigo," I said, instinctively putting up my hands, as if that was going to help.

"You're in big trouble, gringo," he said.

Yes I was, and I didn't like it much. It wasn't the first time someone had pointed a gun at me, but it was the first time the ammo inside it hadn't been water or paint pellets, and I hoped Rodrigo wasn't a firm believer in the saying *"Never point a gun at someone unless you intend to use it."*

"It wasn't my idea, I swear," I said.

"Whatever you say, senor," said Rodrigo.

"They did it all on their own," I said. I wasn't trying to get Jedidiah, Boyd, and the rest of their gang in trouble; I was just trying to get myself out, and didn't care if anyone stepped in to replace me or not.

"You're *the boss*, remember?" said Rodrigo.

"And did your workers always do what you said?" I asked.

"No, but they didn't do anything I *didn't* tell them to do, either," said Rodrigo.

"Well, even if I did tell them to burn your fields, which I didn't, shooting me won't do you any good," I said.

"Wrong; shooting you will do me a lot of good," said Rodrigo. "I'll never get to America now," and with that, he pointed the gun more precisely at my head.

"Wait!" I said, never wanting anyone to stop and listen to me more in my life, and that included every talk I'd ever had with women. "I'll buy your fields for ten thousand dollars," I said, not even bothering to try and figure out if that would be a good deal or not; if it kept me free of holes, it was a bargain.

Rodrigo paused; a few more seconds of life at least. "That's not enough," he said. "My brother wants twenty thousand."

"Maybe, but it will get you off di island to the US," I said. "And I bet your brother will take what he can get."

Rodrigo thought for a moment, then said "What if I say I'm still going to shoot you if you don't give me twenty?"

My tongue became far too bold for its own good once again; it was becoming a habit. Maybe it was a Caribbean pirate thing. "Then I'd say go ahead, because I don't have that much, and you'll be stuck here with a bunch of islanders that are going to hate you for shooting the rum boss and keeping the factory from opening. Again," I said, almost adding that I'd also sure as hell come back as a real ghost and haunt his ass forever.

It took what seemed like an eternity but was actually probably only a few seconds for Rodrigo to lower his gun. "Okay; you win," he said. "I don't like it, but what can I do? When can I have the money?"

"How about tomorrow?" I said. "I'll even call and set up a ride for you with Gus so you can get out of here immediately." It seemed like a good idea to get him as far away as I could as quickly as I could, and now that I was officially the rum boss Gus came more or less whenever

I needed him; a promise of free rum in the future was all that had taken.

"Okay, I'm going to go home to pack so I can get off this cursed island once and for all," said Rodrigo. "I'll be at the bank tomorrow morning at nine."

"Um, that's fine, but remember that Gus won't be here until sometime after noon," I said.

"Damn; you're right. The lazy bastard," said Rodrigo. "Okay, noon, then. And don't try anything funny, gringo. I'll have my Maria here by my side," he said, patting his shotgun.

I liked my Maria a lot better than his; she did the shaking instead of making me shake.

I decided to give up on searching for Billy for the day; I'd had enough adventure for, well, as long a time as I could manage. Some peaceful happy thoughts were what I needed, and a stiff drink. I followed the road the rest of the way east to the Coconut Motel and fetched *my* Maria; I wanted someone to celebrate with. The Rodrigo lockout was over and I wasn't dead yet, two things worthy of a party. And now I was to be the sugar daddy as well as the rum boss.

But I behaved and had only one drink the whole rest of the day and night; one *big* drink, a coconut mug of Pickled Parrot Punch that I kept making the Innkeeper fill whenever it got close to the half way mark (I was trying to cut down). And Maria and I danced later, then passed out together in the back of Black Dog's boat.

And the day ended so well.

"All rums come out of the pot stills as colorless spirits. It's the barrel aging and use of caramel that gives the rum its final color."

Chapter 15

After taking care of business with Rodrigo the next day and making sure he got off di island, I went back to the plantation to look more closely at what I'd gotten myself into this time. The fires had only burned about half the fields before going out, but of course now I wasn't sure if I wanted the other half or not after having talked to Ernesto the day of the fire sale. I immediately put him in charge of my newest business and the decision of which fields to keep; everyone agreed that he was di island expert on sugar cane, and I think it made him at least a little happy to not be working for his wife, Faith, anymore at the factory. We were lucky in that we were entering into a good time of year for planting, and Ernesto promised to immediately hire a full crew back on to clear, replant, and revive whatever fields necessary.

I also purchased Rodrigo's motorcycle and sidecar at the last moment; I probably could have just claimed it after he left since he could hardly take it with him on Gus' plane, but I actually felt the slightest bit guilty about how I'd come to own his plantation. So I gave him two hundred dollars cash; it was a classy old Indian bike, but like everything else I seemed to own these days it needed some tender loving care. I'd always wanted to own a motorcycle but had too highly a developed sense of self preservation to pull the trigger, and now I had one with a sidecar that would make it harder for me to tip over and damage myself. Of course, on di island there weren't thousands of idiots in tank like vehicles waiting to do something stupid and send you road-rashing across the pavement, so perhaps eventually I'd even get brave enough to lose my training wheels altogether and remove the sidecar.

As it turned out I suddenly owned a house, too, on the plantation; not a large one, just a few rooms. But it had a porch to sit on, a bathroom to sit in, and a roof to sleep under, all of which I planned to do in about a week. By which time I figured the cleaning crew would have finally managed to scrub, fumigate, and shovel all traces of Rodrigo out of the building, making it safe enough for me to enter.

After giving Rodrigo his blood money (more like *my* blood money, since that's what it had saved from spilling) my bank account was beginning to look a lot like my rum bottles towards the end of our beach parties; depressingly low. I didn't see how I was going to swing the rest of what we needed and pay the employees. It would be months before we would be ready to distill anything, and months again before any rum would be ready to try and sell. I went over the figures with Luis, Faith, Ernesto, and Cavin, again and again, always coming to the same conclusion; I'd be broke in about nine months, tops.

The 3rd Bank of di island couldn't give me a mortgage on the factory or the fields, since they didn't have that much money themselves, and if I defaulted on the loan all they could do would be to seize the property and try and sell it back to the nearest entrepreneur, which at the moment would just be me again. And I talked to my own bank in Florida as well, but for some reason they weren't too keen on investing in a rum factory on Gilligan's Island (their words, not mine). So for the time being I just went back into my safe mode of ignoring my problems in hopes they would just go away, even though I knew deep down that if I did so for too long my money problems would indeed be gone and I'd have to sweat over starvation and such instead, which wouldn't be much of an improvement in the stress department.

As the next few months went by nothing much changed. The factory continued slowly on course and it was amazing to see how far it had come along. It still had an old school quaintness to it that I loved, like the Wrigley Field of rum factories, but now everything was repaired and ready to produce bottled pirate goodness.

The sugar cane was coming in nicely as well, and Ernesto had managed to rejuvenate many of the plants that had sickly languished under Rodrigo's reign.

And then there was Isabella. Since our little kiss on the beach she'd been extremely scarce, almost as if she was hiding from me. Di island wasn't that big, so I would have thought I'd accidentally run into her more often, but I rarely did so, and the few times I'd seen her she was polite but somehow distant. She was never at Monkey Drool's anymore, either, which made the beach parties a lot less fun, especially during the limbo. I did know where she lived, but I wasn't about to start stalking her; I'd learned my lesson well about that with Polly Lindstrom in the sixth grade.

Luckily, though, I was too busy being frustrated with my failure to get anywhere in my relationship with uncle Billy to be frustrated yet with my lack of one with Isabella. I'd tracked him down on quite a few occasions by now, having finally figured out that he had a sailing route. If he was around in the morning it was usually up on a small hill overlooking the cement industrial docks, watching for ships to plunder, I assumed. In the afternoons I'd sometimes find him inside the bar at Monkey Drool's, drinking rum the Innkeeper would leave out for him like milk and cookies for Santa. And at night he'd wander around and sit upon his broken boat, the Rum Runner, gazing out at the ocean. Where he was

139

the rest of the time and where he slept I still had no idea.

When I did find him he was usually willing to talk a little, although occasionally he would grumble something piratey at me and walk away. I never followed him since I didn't want him to start being wary of me, as I was trying to gain his confidence. But I could never get through to him; our conversations were nonsensical for the most part, and I saw no signs that he knew or understood who I was, or that he even knew who he was.

But I remembered our chat on the night before I decided to stay on di island; it had felt like I'd made a connection that night. Billy had given me the compass that I now carried with me everywhere, and it had come in handy on several occasions when I'd gotten lost exploring. He'd seemed more lucid that evening, and the memory of it made me decide to try an experiment.

I gave Crazy Chester a call and asked him to order me some things on the internet, and he put them on Gus' next flight to di island. I placed them along with a bottle of rum in my backpack and spent the next few days looking for Billy, checking all of his hangouts, and on the third morning I found him watching for ships up above the docks.

I'd come up the hill as quietly as I could to see if he was there first, then backed away into the woods again to prepare. I took off my tee and pulled out my new, red, puffy sleeved shirt and put it and my big belt on, then placed my tri-cornered hat on me head. I felt a little foolish but Billy had responded to my pirate talk that night on his boat, so maybe he would really open up to a full blown fellow swashbuckler. It was worth a try anyway, and at least I'd be ready for Halloween when it rolled around.

I took the bottle of rum out of my backpack, then strolled as boldly as I was able out of the trees towards Billy. "Ahoy!" I said.

Captain Billy jumped, then whirled to face me. He looked me up and down suspiciously, and I was glad he didn't have a sword because he appeared ready to attack this interloping rival pirate. He squinted an eye at me and said, "Who be you, matey; identify yourself!"

Luckily I'd spent some time developing my part; I'd had no intention of going on stage unprepared. "I be Jack Danielson, captain of the Isabella, recently arrived from the port of Key West to make my fortune."

Captain Billy cocked his head. "Captain Jack Danielson you say? I've heard of ye, I think. Be ye any relation to Sergeant James Danielson, the soldier?"

"Aye. James be me father," I said. That was fast; I'd made a connection already, it seemed. I wasn't sure Sigmund would approve of my methods, but I'd gotten through to a little Billy part of Billy, so what did he know?

"Good man, James. Lousy pirate, though; a true landlubber," said Billy. "So what be ye doin' on di island? You said something about seekin' your fortune?"

"Aye, a fortune in rum," I said.

"Ah, rum be liquid gold for sure," Billy said, and he eyed my bottle. "Say, that wouldn't be rum ye be carrying there right now, would it, lad?" he asked, licking his lips.

I looked at the bottle. "Well, so it is!" I said, feigning surprise.

"You wouldn't be interested in sharing that with a fellow buccaneer, would ye?" Billy said.

"Hm," I said, feigning thought (I was good at feigning today). "Share, no."

Captain Billy looked disappointed.

"But I might be willin' to trade it to ye," I said.

Billy's eyes brightened. "What be yer askin' price?" he said.

"Information; I'm looking for someone," I said.

"I'll tell ya what I can," said Billy. "Grab a log and sit down. Who be ye seekin'?"

Now was the touchy part; I didn't want to push Billy too hard. I sat down on one of the logs in the clearing, and said, "I'm looking for a man; his name is

Billy Danielson. He disappeared around these parts some years ago."

Billy stared at me for a long time, then said "Why are you searchin' for this man? Who is he to you, lad?"

"He was my uncle," I said. "And I want to get to know him better."

Billy looked into my eyes, then turned away. "I'm sorry to be the one tellin' you this, matey, but your uncle is gone; he died in a shipwreck many years ago, in the waters surrounding this very island, along with his first mate, Sammy."

"I've heard that story myself," I said. "But I hoped he might still be alive, hiding out here somewhere on di island."

Billy stood up and looked out at the sea. "No, just an old pirate or two be here," said Billy. "I wish I could help ye more; you seem like a good lad. But your uncle Billy is gone."

I wanted to tell him that I knew who he was, and to plead with him to be Billy again. And maybe if I would have kept trying I might have gotten through. But watching him I realized that he was being Billy, just a another version of him. When I'd almost been killed in the accident in what seemed like eons ago, I took a look at who I was and decided to become someone else, which is basically what Billy had done. Yes, he was a pirate; so what? He could be a pirate, and still be my uncle, too, even if he never acknowledged it vocally. Deep down I think he knew, but if he came out and said so it would ruin his disguise, and I decided I didn't want to take that away from him after all. I made a silent vow to try to think of him as Captain Black Dog, my uncle, from that day on.

I stood up and handed Captain Billy Black Dog the bottle of rum. "Thanks. I guess that's what I needed to hear," I said. "Maybe we can get together and talk from time to time; I could use an old salt's advice now and again."

Captain Black Dog gazed at the bottle of Cruzan in his hands, and smiled, then said, "Aye; I'd like that, lad."

I left Black Dog on his hill and went back to modern times. My uncle was a pirate.

I guess I belonged in the Caribbean.

Chapter 16

Over the next few months Captain Billy Black Dog and I had many a long talk. I'd bring him gifts when I could, something good and swashbuckly like a pewter drinking mug, or a pirate flag. He especially liked the bronze spyglass, and the replica and totally safe flintlock pistol I gave him to brandish at people. Then one day, while sitting inside Monkey Drool's, Billy surprised me with a gift.

It was a faded, folded piece of notebook paper that he pulled out of his boot. Its hiding spot made it a little less than desirable to me, and I handled it with care, not wanting to catch some kind of pirate's foot disease.

"That be the map to me swag, lad," said Black Dog.

"I thought you didn't know where your treasure was," I said, examining the map.

"What kind of bloody pirate doesn't know where he buried his treasure!" said Black Dog indignantly.

"Sorry," I said. "But why are you giving this to me?"

"Because, lad, thanks to you I have everything a pirate could ask for," said Billy. "And judgin' by what you've been tellin' me, it sounds like you need my plunder more than I do."

"For what?" I asked.

"Are ya daft? Why, to make the bleedin' rum, of course!" said Black Dog. "Did ya drop a cannonball on your head this mornin', boy-o?"

One thing I'd noticed lately was that the more comfortable Billy became around me the more feisty he seemed to get, and usually at my expense. "Sorry," I said again. "And thank you. It will come in handy, I'm sure."

I'd told Billy about my cash flow problems; not to try and get help from him, since he obviously wasn't in any position to do so, but just to vent. And because he sometimes had a way of putting things in perspective that made me feel better somehow, even if it often involved manning the cannons and opening fire on the governor's mansion.

"Yer welcome," said Black Dog. "But I do have a price; one case of yer finest rum per month."

"That be more than fair, *if* we ever actually produce any," I said.

And that was the end of that for a while. I didn't for a moment take the map seriously. If Black Dog had had any real treasure I wouldn't be trying to figure out how to get the rest of the money together for the factory; he would have opened it himself years ago when he still went by his Billy alias. And a month later I wouldn't have been sitting outside at Monkey Drool's, utterly disheartened at being so close and yet so far from being able to make our first batch. We'd soon have enough sugar, and the factory was ready to produce. But we still had no bottles, labels, or cases, and no money for marketing or shipping. Not to mention enough funds to pay my staff at the factory and the farm for another year while we waited for the first batch of rum to age so we could sell it. I was broke, or at least would be, in about three to four weeks.

"Shit," I said, holding Maria by her base with one hand and making her dance, while gripping a coconut mug of PPP with the other. Both things usually cheered me up, but neither was working today.

"That does about sum it up," said Roger, who had become my closest confidant about the factory, other than Billy. I liked talking to Roger about it because he wasn't directly involved, which made it easier to speak my mind.

"I suppose I could look into selling the place," I said. "Although it's at the bottom of my things I want to do list."

"I've got a wee bit of money I've saved over the years," said Roger. "It's not much, but if it will help..."

"I appreciate the offer, but what's the point? It might get us through a few more weeks, but the result would be the same, and then your money would be gone, too," I said. "Better to just let it end now."

"Shit," said Roger, not so jollily.

I pulled out Black Dog's map. "If only this thing was real," I said.

"What's dat?" said Roger.

I unfolded the piece of paper and put it on the table between us. "Billy, er, Captain Black Dog, gave me this; supposedly it's the map to his treasure."

Roger examined it. "I think I know some of these places," he said.

"You do?" I said, looking at the map.

"Ya, mon. Dis here be that crazy rock that looks like Abraham Lincoln," said Roger, pointing.

"There's a rock on di island that looks like Abraham Lincoln?" I said.

"Well, I tink it looks like John Wayne, but it looks like a person, anyway," said Roger. "And dis be di squid tree."

"I'm not going to ask," I said. "So are you saying someone could actually follow this map?"

"I tink so, laddie," said Roger.

"Are you busy right now?" I said.

"Do I look busy?" said Roger, who only had his Corona to contend with. "What did ya have in mind?"

"Let's go find some treasure," I said. "I think it would be fun to see what Billy has buried there, if anything. And it would take my mind off my impending doom for a while."

"You're on!" said Roger, turning jolly again. "I'll go get a couple of shovels, just in case we find something, and meet you..." and he pointed at the map, "...here. At Black Dog's ship."

"Cool," I said, and it was. I was going on a hunt for pirate treasure; one more thing to cross off my bucket list, although I'd never even put it in my bucket. But now that I was going to do it, I knew I should have always wanted to. Hunt for treasure, treasure the hunt; I was living like a pirate for a day.

We started at the broken Rum Runner. There was a trail marked on the map that led off into the woods away from the ocean, and we found and followed it as it wound its way towards the hills. Eventually it forked on either side of a large rock that looked nothing like honest Abe or the Duke, but was the spitting image of Charlie Brown (but then what rock wasn't?). The map guided us to the left path, and Roger and I trudged up the increasingly overgrown trail until it came to a small clearing.

And there, on the other side, was a giant cephalopod.

In reality it was a Ficus Tree who's roots had grown around another Charlie Brown rock. But they looked very much like tentacles, and the trunk of the tree had broken off, probably in a storm, leaving a sharp, pointy, squid-like head, complete with a big knot for an eye.

The map didn't give us much to go on from there. The X was to the north, but there was no way we could see to go any farther in that direction, unless we climbed the sheer rock wall that ran along behind the tree.

"Now what?" I asked.

Roger was looking at the map, and said "I don't know, mon; there's nothing here."

"Well, if we were ghosts we could float up," I said, looking at the top of the bluff. "Maybe that's how Black Dog does it. Have you ever been up there?"

"No way, laddie. I'm not a fan of heights, so I'm not fond of rock climbing, either," said Roger.

"Well I hate to give up. It's no fun if we don't get the treasure, and it would make for a lousy song," I said. "Let me see the map."

Roger handed it to me, and I held it close and searched every inch. It was a bit of a mess, smudged and stained, making it difficult to discern the details.

"What's this round spot here? Behind the cephalopod?" I said. Cephalopod; you had to love the word.

Roger looked. "I tink dat be Black Dog's lunch," he said.

I examined the small black blotch closer. "Maybe the squid inked," I said. "Should we take a look behind the tree?"

"Aye, we came dis far," said Roger. "Just watch out for di snakes."

I'd learned that much already, having run into the little and not so little slitherers on several occasions since my arrival on di island. I don't know if they were dangerous because I didn't take the time to find out; running the other way seemed sensible, and since snakes didn't have feet they couldn't wear Nikes, so I easily outdistanced them.

I gave Roger the map back (he was the official guide), and he and I each went around the squid on opposite sides and searched our areas. I didn't find anything at first, other than an irritated squirrel monkey who hastened up a tree and swore at me. I was about to tell Roger we should maybe just give up when I spotted something glittering at the base of the cliff wall. I knelt down and examined it, and found it was an empty bottle of Pusser's rum.

"Black Dog's been here," I said, and Roger came over to see what I was talking about. I tried to stand up again by using the vines hanging on the wall for support, but promptly fell through them onto my head.

"Are you alright, laddie?" said Roger.

"Ouch," I said, from my position on the dirty, stone floor.

"There's a cave mouth here behind these vines," said Roger.

"Really? I hadn't noticed," I said, standing and brushing myself off.

We followed the cave through to the other side; it wasn't far, and the light from both ends kept us out of the dark. It led to a small grotto, surrounded by walls on two sides and steep drops on the others; it was a great place for something piratey to be buried.

"I keep expecting Barbosa and Sparrow to leap out and claim the treasure for themselves," I said. "What's next?"

"Now there's just an X marking a spot dat's probably..." he tapered off while looking at the map.

"Well?" I said.

Roger shrugged. "It could be anywhere around here; the map's not exactly to scale," he said. "Should we just start digging?"

"Let's just take a look around before we start excavating the countryside," I said.

We wandered around the grotto, looking for anything out of the ordinary. I found a few more signs of Billy; more empty rum soldiers, a pizza box (evidently he'd plundered some of Gus' imported Italian treasure, too), a pile of beer bottles, and an old copy of Sport's Illustrated's swimsuit issue, which I held up.

"It was probably a Christmas present from di Innkeeper," said Roger.

"A Christmas present?" I said.

"Every year we decorate a palm tree down by Black Dog's boat, and leave small gifts under it on Christmas Eve," explained Roger. "I know di Innkeeper has a subscription just to get dat issue."

We searched some more but still found nothing, other than a hammock between two trees. It was impossible to tell if this was Black Dog's official hideout, but he obviously slept here at least some of the time. "Give me the map again," I said, starting to get annoyed. I had to agree with Roger; it was impossible looking at it to tell precisely where the X was indicating the treasure should be. "This things need coordinates, and it would help if it wasn't so smeared; it almost looks like there are *two* X's, one over the top of the other."

"Two for one treasures?" said Roger with a grin.

"Don't know," I said.

Something was rattling around in the back of my head, trying to get my attention. It kept jumping up and down with its hand raised, but I was busy and ignored it. Finally it disguised itself as Isabella, and I had no choice but to acknowledge it, and when I did, it simply said, "Cerveza."

Isabella was right; I could use a beer. It was hot and I'd been exerting myself for a change, and we hadn't thought to bring water. Mm, beer. Cerveza. If only those bottles weren't empty...

"Wait a minute," I said. "Come here." Roger followed, and I led him over to the pile of old empty beer bottles. "What do you think?"

"About what?" said Roger.

"The bottles. Look at them," I said.

Roger did so, and said, "Aye. Dos Equis. Di Innkeeper used to carry it years ago, but he thought *he* was the most interesting man in the world so he refused to buy any more. What about them?"

"Don't you get it? Dos Equis; two X's. Just like the map; it's not blurred, there *are* two X's," I said excitedly. I felt like Harry Potter solving a mystery, in *"The treasure of Captain Black Dog."*

"Do you tink your uncle is dat clever?" said Roger.

"I tink he's very clever," I said. "Probably runs in the family; he is my uncle, after all. Let's move them."

We did so and found a flat stone underneath. I levered under it with the shovel and Roger lifted it out, and we found a Folger's coffee can underneath.

"This is getting exciting," I said. I pulled the can out of the ground and brushed it off, then removed the plastic lid and looked inside.

"What in it?" asked Roger.

"I'm not sure yet. There are two little bundles in here," I said. I pulled the top one out; it was wrapped in plastic, and rectangular, about the size of a deck of cards, but thicker. I unwrapped it slowly; it was too small to be American money, but maybe some kind of foreign currency...

"What'cha got there, Jack?" asked Roger.

I looked at what I held in my hands. "It's baseball cards. Old baseball cards, in plastic sleeves. They're almost like new." I flipped through them carefully. "Roberto Clemente, Roger Maris, Hank Aaron, Willie Mays, Mickey Mantle, Mickey Mantle, Mickey Mantle..."

"Billy must have liked baseball," said Roger.

I remembered the photo of he and my dad at Yankee Stadium. "Yeah, I guess he did. Geez, there's about ten Mickey Mantles in here. Lots of other big names, too."

"So that's Black Dog's treasure; baseball cards," said Roger. "Too bad it wasn't something more valuable."

I looked at him. "More valuable?" I said. "Do you have any idea how much these might be worth?"

"How much, Jack?" asked Roger.

"Well, okay, I don't know exactly how much, either," I admitted. "But I'm guessing it's a lot; most of them look like they're in mint condition. This could be a small fortune I'm holding in my hands."

"Really?" said Roger. "I didn't know people would pay that much for old cards."

"I know, but human beings are nuts. Remind me to tell you about Beanie Babies some day," I said.

"What else is in there?" said Roger.

I carefully handed him the cards, and he took them the same way. Then I reached into the can and pulled out a round globe, also wrapped in plastic. "Got to be a baseball," I said, unwrapping it. It was a baseball, of an older vintage. "Oh, wow."

"What now?" said Roger.

"It's signed by the Mick," I said.

"Would that be worth something too, then?" asked Roger.

"Oh yeah," I said, chuckling. "But it would depend on whether or not somebody believed the signature was genuine."

"What do you think we should do now?" said Roger.

"I don't know. I wasn't expecting Billy's treasure to actually be worth anything. I'm not even sure he understood when he gave me the map," I said.

"You did tell me dat Billy said to use it to make di rum," said Roger.

"Yeah, he did say that, didn't he?" I said. "Do you think it's right though? Billy's just wandering around di island with nothing but his pirate life for he; maybe we should buy him something with the money instead, like a new boat."

"I don't tink dat's what he would want, lad," said Roger. "It drove him half mad when he didn't get di factory opened years ago; if you want to help him I tink dat's what you should do now."

"Maybe you're right. I don't know if he understands that these are worth something now, or if he just thinks of them as his treasured belongings," I said. "But either way I guess it would help more people if we used it for the factory. Let's put his bottles back and head to base camp."

My first archaeological dig had unearthed some valuable ancient artifacts, and I'd managed to obtain them without a fedora or a whip. Of course, there hadn't been any poison darts, giant bowling balls, or angry natives to contend with, either, just one pissed off monkey, so I didn't know if I was in Indy's league quite yet or not. But like Indiana Jones, my faithful companion Sallah, er, Roger and I, had found a ray of hope in the darkest of hours.

Da da da da, da da da; da da da da, da da da da!

"Distilling the fermented rum removes unwanted components, separating the good from the bad, using heat."

Chapter 17

I didn't really know that much about baseball cards, except that they could be worth a helluva lot of money. But Luis had a pretty good idea; he was from Cuba where baseball is king, and he spent many years after his exile following the American game and collecting a bit himself. And he still had connections in Miami, so when he offered to take the cards stateside and sell them to get money for the factory I took him up on the offer. The Innkeeper thought I was out of my mind to let them out of my sight when they were so valuable, but I chose to trust Luis. Everyone on di island thought very highly of him, and I had something he wanted; a place to make his rum. If he returned he could fulfill his dream at last, and that was a big incentive.

I decided not to sell the baseball signed by Mantle, though; if the cards were worth anything near what Luis had estimated, it would be more than enough to get us over the hump. And I had a feeling that deep down the ball probably meant a lot to Billy, especially if he had been there when Mickey signed it. It would be a physical connection to a memory, one perhaps lost in the dusty and confused catacombs of my uncle's mind, and someday I would give it to him and see if it sparked something.

For now it sat on a shelf in Billy's office, which I suppose was mine now; resting comfortably on an old Doctor Pepper bottle cap, and circled by Sammy's old collar. I knew it would be safe there. In the states I'd have it on a pressure sensitive plate, surrounded by an invisible laser beam alarm system that would confound Cat Woman, guarded by a pit bull who would have no interest in her feline charms. But here on di island, Sammy's aura was protection enough.

While I waited for Luis to return I decided to get to the bottom of the Isabella non-sighting conspiracy. I was convinced now she was avoiding me; there was no other explanation on an island this small. I accidentally ran into my uncle more than she now, and he was a ghost, for crying out loud.

So once again I went off on a quest. It was my third since arriving on di island, the first being for Billy, and the second for his treasure. I was beginning to feel like a hobbit, except I didn't have any jewelry I was trying to chuck into a live volcano.

Isabella wouldn't be that hard to find, if I actually tried. I'd been asking questions about her for months, one per day as to not arouse suspicions, as if there was anyone left on di island who didn't already know I had a thing for her. She worked out of her home, baking papaya, mango, and key lime tarts that she delivered to the market and cantina. I'd eaten them myself on numerous occasion, especially once I discovered she was the one who made them, and they were delicious. All those looks and she could cook, too.

I got up early one morning and drove my motorcycle down to the Crossroads and parked it out of sight. I still had the sidecar connected; I was comfortable enough riding it by now to do without it, but I thought it might come in handy if I came across anyone needing a ride (Isabella). I sat down on a bench outside of the bank, across from the market and cantina, and waited.

Before long Isabella came strolling into sight. She wore a simple yellow flowered dress that looked anything but simple on her, and carried a basket covered by a blue checkered cloth. I noticed she had a purple orchid in her hair, just like my Maria. I watched her go first into the market, then the cantina, and I walked over and stood in the road facing the door, waiting. I knew it smacked a little of the Patty Lindstrom incident, but at least there'd be no one to ground me here on di island.

Isabella came out and spotted me immediately and stopped. She looked like she wanted to run away; it was one of the first times she hadn't seemed to confident for her own damned good, or at least for mine, but she quickly collected herself and walked proudly towards me.

"Are joo following me?" Isabella asked. She was quick; it had taken Patty a week to figure it out.

"Yes, I am," I said.

"Hmpf. Well, what do joo want?" she said.

"I'd like to talk to you," I said.

"So? Go ahead and talk," said Isabella.

"Not here," I said. I didn't want to stand there in island central; we were bound to attract a crowd of onlookers. Di islanders were nice, generous, and all around good people, but I'd found they were also snoopy as hell. "I've got my motorcycle parked by the bank, and I know a place where we won't be bothered."

Isabella looked at me as if trying to judge my intentions, and evidently decided I was safe enough; either that or she didn't care. "Okay, let's go," she said.

We walked over to my cycle and I got on; Isabella hesitated, then got in the sidecar. I soon realized the stupidity of my cycling strategy. When I told her I had my motorcycle she'd agreed to a ride having no idea whether or not I still had the sidecar attached. If I'd had any brains whatsoever in my head she would have been on the seat behind me now as we drove down the bumpy road, her arms wrapped tightly around me. Things like this were the reasons the hottest woman I'd ever had in my life was still my Maria.

I took Isabella to a small secluded beach I'd discovered while searching for Billy. Since then I'd gone there to think on numerous occasions because it was almost always deserted. It was a tiny lagoon surrounded by forest, and the waters were too shallow to be any good for fishing or swimming. It was pretty, though, very serene and unspoiled. And unlike many of the deserted areas on di island it wasn't situated on a cliff, which meant I couldn't throw myself off of anything if the next few minutes went badly.

Isabella looked around, then said "So what did joo want to talk about?"

"I want to know why you've been avoiding me," I said. "The night of my initiation I got the feeling you might like me."

"I do like joo," said Isabella. "But I have been avoiding joo, eet's true."

"Why?" I said.

"Eet's complicated," said Isabella.

"It always is," I thought. I like you, you like me; for some reason that was never enough.

"I made a promise long ago to my mother about who I would marry," said Isabella.

"Marry?" I thought. We hadn't even danced together yet. I had no idea how the relationship could suddenly be moving so fast when I could have sworn it hadn't budged an inch for months; maybe it was a sea turtle and hare kind of thing.

"Let me guess; you're forbidden to marry a gringo," I said.

"Oh, no. Eet's nothing like that," said Isabella. "My mother, she made me promise to marry someone who would take me away from di island to a better life."

"So let me get this straight; you were mad at me when I was going to leave and not open the factory, and now that I'm going to stay and do it you can't have anything to do with me?" I said.

"Jes," said Isabella.

Why did these things always happen to me. "Yeah, that's pretty complicated," I said. "Look, don't you think it might be a good idea to try a date or two first, and if we ever get to the marriage part then worry about what to do about it?"

"I didn't want to lead joo on, since I don't know if I could ever be your wife," said Isabella.

"Lead me on?" I said. "Isabella, I'm not sure I ever even want to get married."

"Joo don't?" said Isabella.

"No. Well, maybe someday, but not right now. And certainly not until my life makes up its mind and goes in more or less one direction for a while," I said. "And besides, what made your mother think a better life was necessarily someplace else? Believe me, someplace else isn't always what it's cracked up to be."

"But didn't joo ever want more than what joo had?" asked Isabella.

"Actually, I discovered I wanted something less. It's more, in the long run," I said. "This is a wonderful life here on di island; you have no idea how much bullshit goes on in the rest of the world. Here you can slow down and take the time to enjoy the good things in life. And yeah, maybe that life is simple, but I'll tell you one thing, there's not much here to make you unhappy, and I think that's the key to happiness."

Suddenly I was trying to convince someone else why they should stay on di island, when I'd almost talked myself out of it months ago. But it was true; my life had been good since my arrival. If Key West had been living in three-quarter time, here it was one-half time, or less. Maybe that would be boring and unfulfilling for some people, like living in the same small town your whole life, but I was beginning to love it.

"But even eef what you say ees true, what about my promise to my mother?" said Isabella.

"Well, again, right now I can't promise I'm ever going to marry you, although you'd be my first and only choice for a wife. But if I did, couldn't I make your life better right here on di island?" I said. "Wouldn't that fulfill your promise, too, or at least part of it?"

Isabella considered this. "I suppose maybe it would be alright," she said. "And I am getting tired of waiting for the right man to come along and take me away from here."

"There's always Crazy Chester," I said. "He lives elsewhere."

"No fisherman!" said Isabella, holding her nose. "Besides, Chester may be the nicest man in the world, but he ees crazy."

"So can we see each other then?" I said.

"Jes. I will be around," said Isabella.

"Good; I'm glad," I said. "And if we ever do get married, I promise I'll take you away from di island for a while. We'll visit Minnesota in January; then we'll see just how long you want to stay in that someplace else."

"He that shall desert the ship or his quarters in time of battle shall be punished by death or marooning." -Pirate Code, agreed by Bartholomew Roberts

Chapter 18

Boyd and I went sailing today, and I ended up buying a house; if I was playing Island Monopoly it felt like I'd own half the board by now.

Boyd had a nice, pretty little skiff with a red, white, and blue sail that I'd seen out on the water on calmer days like this one. The two of us were talking at the cantina over a shared plate of blackened mahi-mahi nachos, when I happened to mention that Jolly Roger had promised to take me on the Crustacean all the way around di island, something I'd been wanting to do. I wanted to see the whole place from the water as part of my full exploration of my new home. I'd covered a large part of it by land, and now I wanted to circumvent it by sea.

Right away Boyd offered to take me instead. It was a perfect afternoon for sailing, and he was planning to go out anyway. And according to him a trip on his skiff would beat the heck out of Roger's noisy, smelly, fish mobile. And he was probably right. I always enjoyed Roger's company, but the quiet rustling of the sails coupled with Boyd's ability to just shut up and enjoy the experience made for a great voyage.

Seeing di island from the water's perspective was very different; it made everything seem much smaller, and the land more finite, which it was. We started from the newly repaired dock system where I'd flown in with Gus, and sailed to the east around the land. I first spotted the small lagoon where I'd taken Isabella, then Monkey Drool's and the Coconut Motel. When we came to Black Dog's grounded boat, Boyd pointed out where the reef was located that had most likely broken her back. It was some distance from shore, and I couldn't help thinking how lucky my uncle was to have survived swimming in storm tossed waters all the way to land, even if his crew hadn't been so fortunate.

We continued on around the north end of di island, past the industrial cement docks and the plantation, and finally around to the west and my factory. It looked pretty sitting up on the hill, sporting it's new coat of yellow paint, trimmed in maroon (my old school colors). We now had tables and chairs with umbrellas on the patio so the staff could sit in the shade on their breaks, and who knows? Maybe tourists visiting the factory one day would do the same, sipping on sampler trays of rum.

Anything seemed possible now. I'd received a call from Luis telling me that he'd sold the cards and gotten a good price; a very good price, actually, even more than I'd hoped for. It turned out that one of the Mickey Mantles was his rookie card; in near mint condition it would have been worth close to two hundred thousand dollars. Unfortunately it wasn't in quite as good a shape as some of the others, but it still fetched a fine price. A two and a half inch by three and a half inch piece of cardboard worth the same as a small house. And people called Chester crazy.

With our financial worries over for a while it was full speed ahead. Since Luis was already in Miami he was going to stop by some wholesalers and personally order the rest of what we needed. I'd gotten out my paints and had been playing around with some ideas for the labels as well as what to call our rum, but I was keeping it hush-hush for now. It looked like it was really going to happen after all, something I never would have dreamed possible a month ago, let alone two years back while sitting in my cubicle on the fourth floor of Image Makers in Minnesota. Life is a funny thing, and mine just kept getting funnier.

Boyd and I were on the southwestern corner of di island, and nearing the completion of our journey, when I spotted a small building sitting on the beach. More like a hut really, wooden walls with a thatched roof. It looked very picturesque; there's just something about a simple hut on the beach in the tropics that's more beautiful than any mansion in Beverly Hills.

"What is that?" I asked, pointing. "Does somebody live there?"

"I don't know," said Boyd. "It's always been there, but I've never seen anyone when I've sailed past."

"Could that be where Billy's been living?" I said.

"Possibly," said Boyd. "Do you want to stop and take a look?"

"Could we?" I said.

"Sure," said Boyd. He steered us close to shore and tossed out the anchor, and we waded the rest of the way to the beach.

There were no signs of any life other than a big iguana who sat watching us on a nearby log. As we got closer I could see the place was a little more neglected than it had looked from the sea, but not bad. One of the support posts on the porch that held the thatched roof up had rotted through, causing it to sag, and the door had fallen off its hinges. Other than that, the place seemed sound.

I went over and peeked in the window; there wasn't much inside the single room, a wooden chair and table, a rotted straw mattress, and a cockatiel that flew out the window over me head, scaring the hell out of me. "Looks deserted," I said.

Boyd pointed. "That looks like it might have been a path, probably to the main road, but it's overgrown now," he said.

"I wonder why nobody lives here," I said.

Boyd shrugged. "It's just a hut. Plenty of them on di island."

"But it's such a pretty spot," I said, and it was. The beach was nice and sandy here, though in need of a good raking, and the ocean's waters seemed particularly green here.

"I suppose it is nice," said Boyd, looking around. "Well, should we get going?"

"Just a sec," I said.

I walked all around the area, examining this rock, that tree, and those seashells. I tried investigating the iguana and his log, too, but he hissed at me like iguanas always did, so I checked out a shrub instead. Finally I went up on the porch and looked out at the teal colored water, then went back over to Boyd.

"How would I go about living here?" I asked.

Boyd looked at me funny, then scanned the area, although I don't think he saw it the same way I did. "You want to live here?" he said. "You already have one of the biggest houses on di island at the plantation. Why would you want this place?"

The truth was I didn't like Rodrigo's house much, and I told Boyd so. Part of it was that it looked like

Rodrigo had picked out most of the furnishings and decorations himself, but that I could change, at least. What I really hated though, was that it was just a house, not unlike any other small home you might find in the states. That and its location. Although the plantation fields ended near the ocean, Rodrigo, or whoever had first built the place, had chosen to put the house in the center of the farm, probably to keep a closer eye on all the workers. Evidently being able to see the water wasn't a big deal to him, but it was to me. Yes, if I stood in just the right spot and looked out the bathroom window at just the right angle I could barely make out the ocean, but that was it. I was finally living in a place where I could afford some beachfront property, and I was damned if I wasn't going to get me some.

"If you're really serious about it I'm sure you could talk to Wonbago," said Boyd. "He'll think you're crazy, but then he thinks all white people are nuts."

I was serious about it, and had been called crazy so many times lately I was in danger of stealing Chester's nickname from him, so that didn't phase me. I was going to live in a hut on the beach and rough it; I'd always have my plantation home to run to if I needed pampering. Although sooner or later I'd probably want to figure out how to get some plumbing and wiring going if I was going to spend much time here.

I tried to remember if I ever saw Thurston Howell the Third or Luvey duck into a latrine, but to no avail; people in the sixties never had to pee, I guess. But I bet the professor hooked everyone up with power for a blender. If he didn't, he should have; with enough boat drinks he might have finally gotten somewhere with Ginger.

I was going to live the beach bum's dream, nutty or not.

Crazy Jack; it had a nice ring to it.

"All roads lead to rum." -W.C. Fields

Chapter 19

I awoke to the sound of the cockatiel somewhere outside my window, and stretched luxuriously in my hut. Sleeping in a hammock everyday had taken some getting used to at first, but I'd become an old pro at it by now. My experimentation with hanging it outside hadn't worked, however; there were just too many things scurrying and going bump in the night for a former city boy to feel safe, and I kept waking up at the slightest sound. But once I moved it inside and hung it between two walls with a roof over my head, I was golden.

I got up and walked over to the window and rolled up the bamboo blinds that were keeping my sun out. The ocean popped into view and I smiled at it like I always did and it smiled back at me. I grabbed a papaya out of the wooden bowl on the table, went outside, and sat on the porch to greet another day.

So far I was enjoying the hell out of this new lifestyle. There were times it was a bit of a hassle not having all the comforts I'd grown used to right at my fingertips, but I was surviving nicely. On a morning like this one I'd get up and take a quick dip in the ocean to rinse away the more advanced civilizations of grime that had arisen during the night. Then I'd walk up the newly cleared path to the road where I parked my motorcycle, which still sported the sidecar, but just for carrying things; Isabella rode behind me now. I'd scoot on up to the plantation, take a shower, and change into some clean clothes, then meet with Ernesto to see how the sugar was feeling today. Then it was off to breakfast at either the cantina or Isabella's house, followed by my morning meeting over coffee on the patio at the factory with the rum three; Luis, Cavin and Faith. And then the rest of my grueling day I'd just wing it.

It was a rough life I'd carved out, and I counted myself extremely fortunate for more reasons than I could count. When I'd left Minnesota to find myself, it was something I made happen; it took an effort to leave everything behind. But this life on di island had more or less fallen into my lap, although if I hadn't left my first self behind to sing my Key West song to begin with, I don't think I ever would have had the nerve to sing this new rum song I was now happily crooning every day. It would have been too big a step to go straight from Minneapolis public relations prisoner to island rum tycoon without being an honorary Key West Conch in between. I don't know that things always work out for the best, but this time at least they'd done a pretty good job, and I was thanking each of my lucky stars.

In fact, life on di island seemed pretty good for just about everyone right now. There was plenty of work to go around, and the tiny economy was booming as Black Dog's baseball card doubloons passed from hand to hand, starting at the factory and plantation and trickling down. There were even a few new immigrants in town as word got around the neighboring islands of the revived job market.

We'd had a decent harvest at the plantation; good quality, although with the replanting of some of the fields it was a bit small. It was enough though, and Luis, Cavin, and Ernesto had overseen the process of extracting and boiling the cane juice to make molasses, which was largely what Luis needed for his first recipe.

And suddenly there was nothing more to wait for, nothing more to prepare. It was almost like a wedding day, except there weren't boatloads of annoying relatives with armloads of toasters, woks, and lawn gnomes arriving down at di island docks. Against all odds it was time at last.

Today we were going to make rum.

It was hard to believe it had been so long since I'd stepped off of Gus' plane. But that was life on di island; time almost had no meaning, no purpose. I used to lament the fact in my old life that all my days seemed the same; here on di island it was what I loved about my life. The difference was of course that the blur of days that passed were enjoyable, flying by like a vacation, instead of trudging along like a time share seminar you got tricked into attending.

I'd made an effort to make what di islanders were calling Rum Day a special occasion, but it was hardly necessary; everyone had been partying leading up to the big morning all week. I kept telling them it would still be a year before we could start bottling the rum but they didn't care, and eventually I didn't either. They were right, as usual. Perhaps the day the rum was ready would be even more meaningful, but that didn't mean we couldn't or shouldn't rejoice in this day too. Life's moments deserve celebrating whenever possible.

Before we got started we gathered together for a little ceremony. Isabella had gotten up even earlier than usual to bake lots of tarts that she brought to the factory for people to nibble on, and I'd had Gus fly in some special *"One Love"* Marley Coffee for a treat. Then we unveiled the new sign above the front doors I'd secretly had made on the mainland, which was just about the *only* way to do or keep anything secret on di island. Chester had brought it with him on the Lazy Lizard when he arrived the day before, and the two of us had hung it up late last night, covered by a tarp. But now I pulled on the rope and the tarp came free, revealing the factory's new name; *"Di Island Rum Company."* It really belonged to di islander's, after all. I was just lucky enough to be along for the ride.

It was Cavin who we choose to add the first pitch of yeast to the fermentation tank, which would turn the sugars in the molasses into alcohol; he was the future of the factory. Then Faith dropped in some more as a nod to all her hard work in getting us organized and open. Finally Luis took over and things got more serious. I watched as he worked, Cavin right by his side, sweating over his creation like a chef in a five star restaurant. He'd been waiting for this for years, for the chance to cook something of his own up, and now he had that opportunity at last and I was happy for him.

The rum that we were starting today wasn't to be his masterpiece, however. We needed a standard rum, too, something that would take only a year to age so we could start getting some income. But Luis also said it wouldn't disappoint, either. We were a small factory and would only produce a few rums to begin with. In time perhaps we could add more storage space and more oaken barrels to age the rum in, but for now there was only so much we could do at a time.

My only regret of that first actual day of production was that Billy wasn't present. I'd tried every pirate trick in the book short of shanghaiing him to get him to the factory, but with no luck. He just didn't seem to like being around a lot of people. I think at least he understood what was happening, though. There was a sparkle in his eye that looked like rum to me, and he just seemed happier. And I like to think maybe he was watching us through his spyglass on some overlooking hill.

Some time later when the fermentation was over and we'd distilled that first batch of rum and put it into the oak barrels to age, I felt a little depressed for some reason. I think it was like post Christmas depression; all the presents had been opened and there was nothing left to look forward to except for next year, which is about how long it would be before the rum would be fully ready. I walked along the rows of barrels, stroking their big round bellies like an expectant father, knowing there was rum inside just waiting to come out.

It truly fit di island lifestyle, this making of the rum. It was a laid back process spanning month after month like the endless tropical summer. And it was like pirate swag, too. You buried it, then came back years later to enjoy it.

Our first treasure was in its chests, waiting to be plundered. The moment of discovery would come when we finally broke off the lock and sampled it, only then to find if there be liquid gold or bilge water inside.

I knew from experience that time flies when you're having rum.

I hoped it flew when you were making it, too.

"Aging of rum is done in oak barrels that have been used to age other liquors. Bourbon barrels are often used because of regulations requiring bourbon makers to use the barrels only once."

Chapter 20

A few months later our rum production was going along smoothly, to the point where we were importing more bourbon barrels and storing them, filled with rum, at the plantation, too. I'd become totally lost in what exactly we were distilling. From what Luis told me in his increasingly terse explanations, it seemed we were making rum to make rum. Something about mixing them together, which I didn't fully understand. But I knew that he knew what he was doing and just stayed out of his way, especially when he told me to get the hell out of the factory and out of his hair before he killed me. Head chefs; they were all the same.

I had a very special project of my own today, one that I'd been unsure about going through with but finally deciding that the time was right. It took some help from Crazy Chester once again; he was always happy to lend a hand and to come to di island, but I wondered if deep down he didn't wish he was signed up in a frequent floaters program with all the trips he'd been making back and forth lately. I sent him on yet another shopping trip, but this time it was important that he find just the right item to make that special someone I was going to give it to happy, and hopefully change their life for the better forever, and cement the bond between us.

Today I was going to propose to Isabella.

Not really, although the thought had crossed my mind from time to time. We'd been getting along very well together, except for the rare occasions when she would find some reason to release her Latin temper at me. Then she was like a tempest, beautiful and wondrous to behold, and dangerous as hell to be around until she calmed down. But she was worth every hailstone and ceramic vase she threw my way, and when the sun came out after the rain it was always worth my having gotten a little wet.

But today was all about Captain Billy. I had yet another present to give him, one I'd had in mind almost since the day I'd discovered he was my uncle, and still alive. I'd been somewhat reluctant to go through with it, though. I felt it was possible it might do him more harm than good. But it was Isabella who finally talked me into it, saying that everyone yearns for love, including those that have lost it and are in pain because of it; they perhaps even more than others, though they may swear otherwise. Considering the fact we were talking about a crusty old pirate ghost, I thought she was being a little sappy, but I knew what she meant and agreed with her, and knew enough to keep my mouth shut or risk unleashing Calypso again.

Once Chester had arrived with the surprise we spent the day looking for Black Dog, but didn't find him until the following evening, seated up on his old boat. I'd been hoping we could corner him in one of his other hangouts; I was worried there may be too many bad memories associated with the Rum Runner that could take what I was trying to do in the wrong direction. Billy was often more somber around the wrecked vessel, more thoughtful. I suppose I would be too if I were to see my old mangled Suburban.

It had never occurred to me before, but both Billy and I had had our lives changed by crashes; one of us into a reef, and the other into a semi. I guess that's what too close a look at mortality can do to you, make you look at the life you have and decide what the hell to do with the rest of it. It's too bad that's what it often takes to make positive changes; we shouldn't have to risk those very lives to realize we're missing out on living. Maybe we could receive a wake up call from a desk clerk in the sky from time to time, to get us to open our eyes and stop sleeping the years away.

As for Black Dog I'd decided ahead of time to go through with my plan even if he was at the boat; obviously I wouldn't have been checking to see if he was there and keeping Chester away from Monkey Drool's and a cold drink otherwise. If that's where it was meant to happen then so be it. I didn't believe in fate as in my life was already written; it was a depressing thought, like we were just going through the motions. But I was beginning to see that a thing happening one way and in one place as opposed to it happening slightly differently, or not at all, was liable to cause all sorts of other things to change down the road as well. It was almost silly to try and figure out the consequences of your actions; you could decide to go out for chili dogs instead of the usual hamburgers one night and end up playing professional Mahjong in China a month later because of it. The best a person could do was to try and have some fun and not act like an asshole most of the time, and just go with the flow.

So while Chester stayed behind in the trees, I walked out onto the beach and into Black Dog's view; he spotted me immediately and stood up and waved from the ship's rail. "Well if it ain't Captain Jack," he said.

"I told you, I'm not a captain anymore; I'm a merchant in the rum trade now," I said.

"Once a captain, always a captain," said Black Dog. "Are ye comin' aboard?"

"Not yet," I said. "I was hopin' ya might be able to help me with something."

"Oh?" said Black Dog. "What's wrong, lad, are ya havin' problems with that bonnie wench of yers again? She still too much for ya to handle, is she?"

I'd made the mistake of discussing a spat Isabella and I had had with Billy, and I still hadn't heard the end of it. It seemed to delight him to no end, especially the part where she dumped the bowl of tart batter on my head.

"No, I'm not in trouble with Isabella, and yes, she's still more than I can handle," I said. "And no, I don't care. Anyway, it's someone else who's in trouble this time, another sailor. Can ya come down and meet him?"

Captain Black Dog looked reluctant to move; he was wary of people he didn't know, suspicious like any pirate trying to steer clear of capture should be. "I don't know, mate. I'm not sure it's a good idea for me to leave me ship right now what with this weather," he said.

The weather was fine, as usual, at least in my world. Billy loved to drum up a good storm in his noggin as an excuse for whatever it was he was trying to avoid at the moment, but I knew how to clear the skies in a hurry, and held up my bottle of Coruba. "I've got rum," I said.

Black Dog looked up at the stars. "Never mind, it's a red sky at night after all," he said, then climbed over the railing and walked over to me. "Ya could have mentioned the rum to start with and saved us a lot of blathering."

"Sorry," I said, and handed him the bottle. He opened it and took a good swig from it, and said "So what's the situation, matey? We rescuing someone from the town jail? Kidnapping the governor's daughter? Or is it just standard pillagin', plunderin', riflin' and lootin' we be about this evening?"

"No, there's just a pirate in port without a home. I thought you might give him a bunk," I said.

"Me? Look, lad, you know I'm a lone wolf," said Black Dog. "I don't take kindly to strangers, and I don't need to play nursemaid to some dry behind the ears swabby who can't even find a bed on his own."

"How about a wet on the nose sailor's mate?" I said.

"Wet on the nose? You been drinkin' seawater again, have ye?" said Black Dog.

I whistled, and somewhere in the trees Chester let go, and the four legged able seaman came bounding across the sand towards us.

The young black lab greeted me, then discovered Black Dog and a plethora of new things to smell, and proceeded to circle around him excitedly. The captain looked down at him, standing in the stocks still as the dog checked him out, then said hesitantly "W-w-where did you find him?"

"He was wandering around alone by the docks. I'm guessing one of the sailors bringing that shipment of bottles marooned him; probably a Frenchman," I said.

Billy nodded vacantly, still watching the lab, who jumped up on him, evidently happy with the variety of scents he had to offer. "He seems kind of lonely," said Billy.

"I was thinking the same thing," I said. "I don't think he'd mind if you petted him."

Captain Billy reached down, his hand trembling slightly to pet the pooch, but the dog licked him before he could finish. Billy jumped, but it seemed to please him, and he knelt down on one knee so he could commune with his new acquaintance properly. "Does he have a name?" he asked.

"Not yet, and like I said before, he doesn't have a home, either. And I can't keep him; Isabella is allergic to dogs," I said, which wasn't entirely true. Isabella in fact liked dogs very much, and if she was allergic to anything it was their hair in her house while she baked. It was only a white lie, though, and hardly a sin next to the public relations whoppers I'd told over my years of working for the evil empire. "Can he stay with you for a while until we find him a new owner?"

"Hm? What's that, lad?" said Billy, totally engrossed in the dog, who in turn was totally engrossed in Billy's scratchings behind his ear.

"Can you take care of him for now?" I said again. "No one seems to want to do it, and he shouldn't just be wandering around di island by himself. It probably won't be for long; Gus will most likely take him off your hands the next time he shows up. He's been talking about getting a copilot for quite some time now."

"Gus take him? And have him fly around with him in that damned fool contraption of his?" said Billy grumpily. "Not on your life, lad. A sailor's feet should be on the ground or in the water, not floatin' in the sky waitin' for a cannonball."

Which was the only reason I'd mentioned Gus, of course; Gus hated dogs. But Black Dog hated Gus, too, or at least his plane. "Well, if there was anybody else..." I said.

"He can bunk with me for now," said Billy.

"It might take some time to find him a new home," I said.

"That's okay, lad," said Billy, now rubbing the dog's belly as he rolled on his back in the sand (the dog, not Billy). "We'll just see how it goes. You know, he sort of reminds me of me old first mate."

What a coincidence. "I've got some things back in the woods that might make it easier to take care of him.

Food, a couple of bowls, a few toys, and a leash," I said. "I'll go get them and then I gotta run. Are you two gonna be okay?"

"Aye, we'll be fine. He's got salt in his blood, I can tell," said Captain Black Dog.

I went back and got the bag of dog goodies from Chester and left them with Billy; he'd find Sammy's old collar in there eventually along with a new one, and it would be up to him to decide which he wanted to use.

It was hard to tell if I'd done my uncle any good; Captain Black Dog seemed to like his first mate, but how the Billy part hiding inside him felt was hard to tell. But I guess if it made either of them happy it was a good thing, so I was glad I'd gone through with it. And at the very least my uncle would have someone to keep him company now.

Two days later I woke up in my hut as usual and headed outside to swim in my ocean. But as I walked sleepily through the door I tripped over something, sending me sprawling headfirst into the sand. I swore, although it wasn't easy with a mouthful of beach, then stood up and went back to find out what had face planted me.

It was an old guitar case, laid out lengthwise across the doorway for maximum tripping efficiency. Why it was on my porch I had no idea; I hadn't been whooping it up the night before so there was no reason for Cavin to have left it there after one of my *"Bonfire on di Bosses Beach"* parties. As I looked at it though I realized it wasn't even Cavin's case; he used a soft sided one to tote his prized possession around.

I knelt down and opened it, trying to make some morning sense of things; ideally I liked to have my morning cup of island coffee before I started tripping over mysterious musical instruments. There was a well seasoned guitar inside the case, scratched and worn, and missing a couple of strings. A piece of paper was stuck between the remaining strummers, and I pulled it out and opened it.

It was a note, and I recognized Billy's chicken scratchings immediately. It said, *"This used to belong to your Uncle Billy; maybe you can take some lessons and use it to play that song of yours you keep going on about."*

And it was signed, *"Captain Black Dog and First Mate Sammy."*

It was the best gift I'd ever received.

"So kick back, relax, and be merry!" -The Rum Bible,
Rum Barrel Bar in Key West, Florida

Chapter 21

It was Crazy Chester's birthday, and all hell was breaking loose.

I'd been planning a party for him for weeks, ever since he let slip about ten times that his big day was coming up. Chester wasn't one of those people who tried to keep their birthday a secret, or told everyone they didn't want a party. It was his birthday, damn it, and he wanted attention and merriment, which I think deep down is what those other people want too, but are afraid sometimes to show.

And I was always happy to have an official reason for a good time. There was nothing wrong with non sanctioned festivities; it would be ridiculous, not to mention terribly boring, to only have fun when the calendar said it was okay. But for a real get down and boogie, tap that keg, throw the pig on the spit, and get frisky with anything that moved blowout there was nothing like a birthday, wedding, or Leif Erikson Day, to get everyone off their lazy arses and onto the same party page. And I hoped Crazy Chester's bornday would be just such an occasion.

My original plan had been to have the party at Monkey Drool's as always. There was a bar and music, and a beach that was coincidentally situated right next to an ocean, perfectly placed for spontaneous skinny dipping. And the bar also had plumbing, which when any number of women were involved beat my Robinson Crusoe style bungalow.

But it was now hurricane season, and while we didn't have Larry, Mary, or Nathaniel bearing down on di island, we did have a few days of rain settling in. The small inside bar at Monkey Drool's would never do for a fete of this magnitude, so I decided to hold it at the factory.

Chester's birthday fell on a Friday, which always made things just a bit wilder since almost no one had to work the next day. Actually, *no one*, and not almost no one, had to work since this was di island. And if Geeah and Terrance at the cantina or Akiko over at the market didn't feel like coming in on a Saturday, or any other day for that matter, then the cantina or market didn't open. Nobody got bent out of shape because they couldn't get their banana pancakes that day or their paperclips, and somehow we survived the hardship of not having a store and restaurant that were open three hundred and sixty-five and a quarter days a year.

I gave all my workers the afternoon off at the factory and plantation the day of the party. For one thing I needed everyone out of the way at the factory so I could decorate, and for another, I needed their help in doing it. And I wanted the party guests to be able to show up by late afternoon so we could have a cookout before the rain's scheduled arrival in the evening.

I'd been missing manning my own grill for a long time now, having not done so since leaving Minnesota. So I'd had Jedidiah build a nice, big, brick one in the corner of the patio as part of my preparations for the rush of turistas that were sure to come to di island once they'd tasted our rum. We still hadn't produced even an airline bottle of the stuff yet, but I was already dreaming of hungry foreigners paying over-inflated prices for jerk chicken and hamburgers. And for boat drinks from the bar in the other corner that was still in the planning offices of my head.

I think I hurt the Innkeeper's feeling when I asked Crazy Chester to bring some kegs of Landshark with him on his boat (which was technically illegal, but Chester was also a pirate and didn't mind engaging in a little harmless smuggling). Monkey Drool's didn't have tap beer, and I felt there was nothing like tapping another keg to keep the party rolling. Francis got over it anyway when I paid him to bring some of his Pickled Parrot Punch, and as a special throwback treat, a batch of his Big Banana Brew. I wasn't quite sure how I was going to mend the fences when he found out about my aforementioned patio bar, since he was known to hold grudges, but I'd worry about that when it happened. Until then I'd taken to calling him the most interesting innkeeper in the world to get farther onto his good side before the rum hit the fan.

I'd grown fond of saying that when people said it was five o'clock somewhere they were talking about di island, as if whenever it was five o'clock here it was every other time in the world simultaneously. So when Chester's party started at five o'clock, it meant that in a way everyone for that day was saying *"It's Crazy Chester's birthday somewhere."* At least that's my story, and good luck proving me wrong.

I was actually a little nervous; I'd gone out of my way to try and make this a memorable night, not just for my good friend, but for all of my good friends. I'd even had invitations printed, something it turned out Mr. Wonbago could do out of one of his many offices (I don't know if he had an official printer's coat too or not). I'd given one to every islander I could find so that all would feel welcome to come, though I knew not everyone would be there; just like any other community there were those who preferred a quiet night at home. But I hoped for a good turn out so I could give something back to di islanders.

I'd stationed Boyd up on the roof with a big box of beads to throw to arriving guests, but only after finally winning my argument with him that the women didn't need to show any particular parts of their anatomy to get a string (Boyd was from New Orleans). Roger and I manned the grill, serving up grouper, beef, and jerk on a bun. It took a while to get everyone fed, but they didn't seem to mind, and I didn't either. I had an apron on my body and a spatula in my hand once more, and this time Brittany wasn't making me grill veggie burgers.

We were just wrapping up the dinner hour when the first raindrops began to fall, and once we'd moved the party inside the festivities really began. Cavin and Boyd were going to play music for the first few hours, then the DJ would start; the DJ being my iPod on shuffle, that is. One of the first things I commissioned once we had money to spend on things that weren't absolute necessities, was a sound system for the factory and patio. I'm a firm believer in the power of music to make all parts of life more enjoyable, including work. In fact, I'm thinking about having a chip installed in my head so I can have a soundtrack play as I go through my day. That way when I see the ocean I can have a Buffett song pop on, and when I start jammin' Bob Marley will jam right with me. And maybe Old Blue Eyes can help get me in the mood with Isabella, although I'm not sure I can fit any more mood in that department than I already have.

But for now outside my head it was Cavin on the guitar and Boyd on his bongos as usual; they didn't need my amateur stumbling fingers helping them, although thanks to Cavin's lessons I was now able play Jingle Bells on my own guitar without setting the local wildlife on edge.

About an hour into their show we got a surprise, when Cavin went into the crowd and found Akiko and dragged her into the corner where they were playing. Akiko was from Japan, but had moved to the states and earned a business degree at Michigan. She also earned a husband, Mark, and together they opened a small corner store in Detroit. But after the third robbery in a year they'd both had enough, and Mark, a devout Parrot Head, talked Aki into moving to di island to get away from it all. They bought the deserted clothing store at the Crossroads and turned it into a general market, and were very happy until Mark passed away a couple of years ago. Akiko stayed, having fallen in love with di island and Mark's dream.

Aki was a cute, petite little thing in her thirties, but it was impossible to tell exactly where since she never seemed to age. Since I'd been on di island she had always kept pretty much to herself, perhaps because of Mark's death. But lately I saw more and more of her and she seemed like a different person, ready again to be a part of the world, and to find a new song to sing.

And as it turned out, did she ever have a voice to sing it with when it came to her. I don't know how Cavin knew about it; I had no idea myself, and by the looks on the faces of my fellow islanders in the factory, I doubt if anyone else knew, either. But then again she had shown up at one of my bonfires, and as usual Cavin and his guitar had been there. And because of Luis and a fifteen year old bottle of Diplomatico rum he had picked up in Miami and insisted upon sharing with me, I was there only in spirit, or more precisely in my spirits, from ten o'clock or so on. If Jedidiah had suddenly pulled a saxophone out of his back pocket and blown a Clarence Clemons like solo I wouldn't have remembered it.

Akiko was shy and stumbling at first, and I had a hard time hearing her. But by the time she got to her third song she was making Marley smile, and when she helped us all set sail with Captain Black Dog ala Garth Brooks, she became a bona fide little ham.

As for the birthday boy, he was in full crazy mode, which meant he was hell bent on having a good time. The fist pumps into the air had begun, and he'd been dancing since Cavin had first started tuning his guitar. I couldn't say for sure exactly who Chester was dancing with however, but if I would have had to guess I would have said every woman in the building.

I took a few turns with Isabella as well. I'd given up all hopes of looking like anything but a spastic, short circuiting robot on roller skates compared to her. I was just out of her league, meaning I'd been kicked out a long time ago and sent back down to the minors. We both had rhythm, the difference being her whole body had it while mine ended at my extremities. I could bob my head, clap my hands, and stomp my feet to the music with the best of them, but if I tried to bring my torso into the mix there was no team spirit. So I just enjoyed watching Isabella shimmy and undulate between PG and PG-13, with a few moves dangerously close to R.

After the Rum Trio (so dubbed later by Gus) finished to rousing applause, I plugged my iPod in and the lights went out. Don't ask me why, they just went out. The storm outside wasn't that bad, just rain, and shouldn't have caused any outages. Perhaps whoever was manning the tiny power plant that evening wanted to join the party and just threw a switch. Or maybe the goats chewed through a cable once again. And it was entirely possible that di island wasn't Mac compatible. All I knew was we were standing there in the dark, and the party appeared to be over.

And that was when hell began to break loose from its moorings.

I heard Chester do a *"Woo-hoo!"* a minute or so after the darkness fell, and then his head lit up. He'd been wearing this festive and ridiculously gaudy hat all evening, perched precariously on his small cranium. He looked like a Parrot Head version of Chiquita Banana, fins, feathers, and margaritas piled up to the sky. And as it turned out it lit up, too, although being Crazy Chester it had taken the lights going out to remind him to turn it on. But his timing was perfect; it was like plugging in the Christmas tree for the first time every year. The crowd oohed and aahed, then clapped. I think they thought the whole thing had been planned, but with Chester things just worked out that way.

Boyd still had his bongos within reach and started playing a conga beat, and Chester started dancing around again, his hat bouncing up and down in the darkness like the ugly little spud from Ghostbusters. A conga line soon formed behind him, and Chester the bright headed raindeer led everyone, including myself, out the patio door and into the rain.

The water falling from the sky was still warm, and there was something wonderfully exuberant about dancing and stomping around the patio in it. Boyd jumped up on the wall and kept the beat going, and eventually the conga line broke up and turned into a wild drum dance, an island version of a rave, a sea of frolicking islanders bouncing up and down in the rain.

Suddenly Gus emitted a primal scream, sounding his barbaric yawp, then ripped off his denim shirt and went running headlong towards the ocean. By the time he left land he'd ripped off everything else as well, something I didn't really need to see. But within a few moments a small group of di islanders had joined him, splashing around in the sea like happy naked porpoises.

The last I saw of Chester that night he was off in a corner dancing with Akiko, which didn't really surprise me. He'd always spent more time shopping in her market than any male of our species should, and just how many *"I Love Di Island!"* tee shirts can one man not wear? If something came of it I'd be happy for him, and for Aki; he was a nice guy as far as lunatics went. I just hoped his head wasn't going to short out in the rain and give them both elctroshock treatments.

And me? I ended up somewhere south of my factory on the beach with Isabella. If I remember right the idea had been to walk along the shore to my bungalow, which was doable if you didn't mind wading a bit. But something had gone right along the way, and we didn't quite make it that far before stopping for some R&R (and R).

I awoke the next day in my hammock with a still slightly wet Isabella in my arms, and sand stuck in all sorts of unusual places on my person; but it had been worth every irritating little grain. I'd like to say exactly what happened, but I'm a gentleman and I don't kiss and tell (much). In this case though I was sorely tempted to go and find a mountaintop and shout all about it, then start a Facebook page on the subject, and hire a film crew to do a documentary.

But I wouldn't be able to do it justice in any form of media, so I'll just leave it at it was the greatest three hours of my life. And yes, I'm bragging now. Not to mention exaggerating. Greatly.

But I don't think I'd be exaggerating if I said Chester's party was a success.

"Such a day; rum all out. Our company somewhat sober; a damned confusion amongst us! Rogues a plotting." -Blackbeard

Chapter 22

It wasn't Crazy Chester's birthday but all hell was breaking loose anyway.

It was still hurricane season, and this time we did have the next alphabetical alternating male and female name bearing down on us. She wasn't going to hit us straight on, thank the tiki gods, but the glancing blow she was smacking us with was quite enough.

I'd been in plenty of storms before, and not just the *"Damn, I said something stupid to Isabella again"* kind. I was from Minnesota, where the weather could drum up all sorts of petty nastiness at a moment's notice. That was the one and only advantage I could see to hurricanes; at least you got some proper warning it was on the way to visit you. When a tornado siren finally went off you were liable to still be sitting on your living room sofa, a thousand feet in the air, and well on your way to visit the great and powerful Oz.

But a hurricane wasn't as short lived as a tornado, either. Yes, if a tornado formed and went through your neighborhood it was a terrible thing to behold, but the damage was mostly confined to near where the juggernaut went through. With a hurricane it often created a swath of damage the width of a small continent, and when it arrived, it settled in like a Jehova's Witness who had somehow penetrated your household defenses. And it was just as capable as a tornado of rearranging the area into something Picaso-like, just usually not with a single, quick, knock out punch.

Most all of di island buildings had been standing for years and had already survived full on tropical assaults from Mother Nature. But the boats at the docks were always vulnerable, so some of the captains, including Jolly Roger, were sailing to Crazy Chester's Bar and Boat Stop in the Keys, which weren't supposed to get hit. The factory, along with most of the businesses on di island, was shut down, storm panels in place. Luis assured me that everything would be fine, but I feared for the safety of my precious rum, which was getting tantalizingly close to its first birthday.

I worried about my uncle Billy as well, but not as much as I had a week or so ago. I'd told Billy as much, that with the hurricane coming he and Sammy should stay with me at the plantation, but he refused. This time though I wouldn't back down when he said they would be safe, and demanded proof. I didn't expect him to comply, but he surprised me by taking me along the paths that Roger and I had followed while looking for his treasure, all the way up to the cave that had led to the grotto where it had been buried. We went inside and just to the right of the entrance, hidden back in the shadows, was a tunnel Roger and I hadn't seen. Billy and I followed it and it led to a cozy little cavern. This was Captain Black Dog's hideout, and the fact that Billy was revealing its secret location to me showed just how far we'd come, and it meant a lot to me. I used Black Dog's pirate trust level as a barometer for my relationship with my uncle, and this was the ultimate show of faith.

Billy's cave was actually pretty danged nice, at least when it came to caves. He had another hammock stretched out between two stalagmites (stalactites? I could never remember which was which), and Sammy had a big bed right next to it made of old cushions. It was cool, and the area was lit by a few lanterns, giving it a soft glow. And my uncle had a nice collection of belongings, gathered throughout di island and Christmases past, I'm sure; everything from decorations to furniture to books, and on to a nice little pantry full of canned goods and sodas.

I had no idea where he got it all; probably from the generosity of di islanders, but I didn't worry about him nearly as much after seeing his hideout that day. He had it better than I did at my hut, if you took away my beach, ocean, and thatched roof, that is. And the cave would be more than safe against the coming hurricane, provided he didn't go outside to bellow at it, pirate style.

I got a bit of a shock when Isabella announced she was going to travel to the Keys with Roger; I'd been looking forward to holing up with her until the storm passed at the plantation with lots of strawberries and rum, hoping we'd find some way to pass the time. Faith was going with her, and the two of them had a girl's week planned, heading eventually down to Key West. Akiko was tagging along, too, but I had the feeling from listening to the coconut telegraph rumor mill that she would be spending most of her time with Chester; there seemed to be something crazy going on there. I wanted desperately to go along as well; my Isabella was off to visit my Key West, and without me. But she made it perfectly clear I wasn't welcome; she wanted an adventure alone with Faith, and I wasn't going to pout. Much.

So by the time the storm arrived I was all alone and left to entertain myself. Luckily the Innkeeper was running a monsoon package at the motel and bar, a room and all the beer you could drink, for anyone who wanted to party like a hurricane without risking life and limb. Which was good, since the winds were already whooping it up by the time I made my way over to Monkey Drool's. Of course I wanted to party like a hurricane; I was a big supporter of that sort of thing, and I had nothing better to do now that the love of my life was off to visit Key West. My beautiful, exotic, Latin hula girl, on her own in the big town, mingling with rich turistas from New York and horny young sailors...

I was trying not to think about it, which obviously wasn't working so well. But if Isabella wanted to have some fun on her own, I was all for it, and trusted her completely. I just didn't trust anyone in the Keys with a Y chromosome, except for Roger and Chester, and perhaps some of the men at La Te Da's in Key West, although even they might be tempted to reconsider a few things after seeing my Isabella dance.

This was only going to be the second time I'd drank in the Shrunken Head Lounge since it had been renamed for the new tradition Jedidiah had inadvertently started one day. I'd been outside painting a picture of Monkey Drool's from the beach when a storm suddenly came up, causing everyone to scurry inside. We sat bored for a while, and there was this empty coconut shell (there always seemed to be an empty coconut shell nearby on di island). Jedidiah took it and asked if he could borrow my paints, and sat in the corner drawing a face on it. When he was finished, we all agreed it looked like the Innkeeper (except the Innkeeper), who was exactly who Jed had been trying to capture; it turned out he had some artistic talent he didn't even know about.

The Innkeeper wasn't very pleased at first, especially with the sewed shut mouth ala a shrunken head (Francis had been going on and on again about how interesting he was). But soon everyone else in the place wanted one too, and weeks later there were shrunken heads hanging by twine all over the ceiling. It was kind of a pain in the ass because they hung so low that everyone but Ernesto kept bumping into them, but at least then you got to chew out someone's head.

I was the last of the lounge lizards to arrive for this evening, and the usual crew of miscreants were already there; Cavin, Ernesto, Luis, Jedidiah; and the not so usual, Mr. Wonbago. Gerald never came to our parties and very rarely to Monkey Drool's, so I was surprised to see him out on such a storm tossed night. But that was exactly why he *was* there; I guess most people have a certain something that will drive them to drink, and with Wonbago it was hurricanes, which he was truly scared to death of.

Another surprise guest I hadn't expected was Gus Grizwood; I'd have thought he'd be miles away from here by now. He'd have to be insane to fly into an area about to be hit by a hurricane, unless he was looking to collect some insurance.

I took a seat across from Gus. The center of the long table was filled with iced down buckets of beer; if you were in the bar tonight it meant you'd paid for the package, and you could just help yourself to a bottle. Which I did, reaching for the Kalik as always when it was available.

"What are you doing here?" I said in an almost accusatory tone, still untrusting of anyone male.

"There's a hurricane outside; where the hell else would I be?" said Gus.

"Someplace else, maybe?" I said. "You do own a plane, don't you? I just figured you'd fly out of Dodge before the posse stormed into town."

"I've ridden out every Caribbean hurricane for the past six years in this bar, and I'm not about to stop now," said Gus.

"Don't you worry about your plane?" I said.

"All the damn time," said Gus. "But right now it's reasonably secure inside a hangar in Kingston; I got a ride here from Jarek."

Jarek was another seaplane pilot who flew in the area, based out of Jamaica. "So you consider this bar to be safe in a hurricane, then?" I said.

"Hell, no. This thing is liable to fly apart any second now like a Lincoln Log cabin kicked by a three years old," said Gus. "But if I'm gonna die, I'd rather it be here."

"That's comforting," I said.

"Can we talk about something else, mon?" said Wonbago.

"Do you be a little nervous, Gerald?" said Jedidiah with a wicked grin. "Be cool, mon; there's noting to worry about. It's only a category two hurricane.

Dat means maybe some rain, maybe some hail, maybe some one hundred mile an hour winds..."

"I'm going to revoke your citizenship when I get back to di office," said Wonbago.

"*If* it's still standing," said Jedidiah.

Wonbago didn't actually have much to worry about, though. The winds were only whipping at about fifty miles an hour on di island. *Only* fifty.

"So what are we going to do to pass the time tonight?" asked Cavin.

"You mean, besides drink?" said Gus.

"Yeah, besides that," said Cavin.

I counted. "Not enough to play baseball," I said.

"Too many heads in the way, anyway," said Luis.

"Does anybody know any good drinking games?" asked Cavin.

"I do; pick up your beer and drink it. You win, so drink another," said Gus.

"We could use some music, for starters," I said. The place was way too quiet, especially for a bar.

"Si, where's the boombox?" asked Ernesto.

"I'll go get it," said the Innkeeper, probably wishing someone would have thought of it before the rains and wind started. He disappeared through the backdoor that led to the outside portion of the bar.

"So how's the rum doing?" I asked Luis.

"The same as it was doing yesterday when you asked me, and the day before that, and the day before that, and the day before that," Luis answered, somewhat irritably.

"Then we're still on schedule?" I said.

"Yes, and that's not going to change, so you don't need to keep asking. It's good rum right now, and it will be good rum in a week when we open the casks. But we need to wait until it has officially been aged for one year," said Luis.

"Sorry, I'll stop asking," I said.

"Thank you," said Luis.

We all sat quietly waiting for the music to arrive.

"So how are the other rums doing?" I asked.

Luis looked at me, then got up and went to the bar and got *di stick*, then walked over to my shrunken head and rapped it a good one.

"Ouch," I said. It was another tradition that had arisen; if someone was irritated with you, they could hit your head with *di stick*, and you were supposed to react in pain, voodoo style.

The Innkeeper returned with the boombox, and said "Di storm is blowing pretty good now. Gonna be easy to get more coconuts for di heads; dey gonna be lyin' all over di ground." He plugged in the boombox and hit play, and Kenny Chesney popped on. I'd burned some CDs on my laptop for the bar, having had enough of radio and commercials. Someday I'd see if it was possible to get XM on di island, so we could get us some Margaritaville Radio.

"That's better, dude," said Cavin. "Still bored, though."

"That's because there's no women," said Jedidiah

"No, that's what's nice," said Gus. "Just us men."

"Is there a deck of cards?" asked Luis.

"No, mon; most of dem blew away last week in di storm," said the Innkeeper.

"Oh, well," said Gus. "Guess we'll just have to drink. Gonna get bored with beer, though."

"I know where there's some rum," I said.

"Don't even think about it," said Luis. "You may be di boss, but touch di rum and I quit."

"Fine, be that way," I said. I wasn't really serious about it anyway; I think. "You're the one who told me it was good rum now."

"Too bad this isn't one week later," said Cavin. "Now that would be a party."

Yes it would be; I'd just cart a barrel over here and tap into it. Rum straight from the barrel during a hurricane...

"Stop tempting him," said Luis. "Drinking the rum before it's ready is a sin."

"So is all the really good stuff," said Gus.

"We'll wait," I said. "Luis is right, and besides, it wouldn't be fair to everyone who isn't here."

"We'll see if you still feel that way after we all die tonight," said Gus.

"Good point," I thought.

"Then what are we going to do to liven things up?" said Cavin.

I thought about it. "I have an idea..."

"Pour together 4 oz dark rum, 2 oz lemon juice, 2 oz passion fruit syrup, shake with ice, and strain into a hurricane glass over ice." -Hurricane drink recipe

Chapter 23

"Ow!" said Gus. He picked up a glass of beer from the table, drank it down, then pulled the steel tipped dart out of his head. "Jack," he announced, and chucked it at my head. He missed, and picked up another glass of beer and drank it, too.

I picked the dart up off the floor and looked around, then said "Luis," and threw it, and it stuck in its target.

"Ouch," said Ernesto.

"What are you saying ouch for?" I said.

"Because that was my head you hit, not Luis', boss," he said.

"It was?" I said.

"Si," said Ernesto, and Luis nodded in agreement.

"Ruling?" said Gus.

It was my game, and my rules, some of which I was still making up as we played. "Do you have any tequila back there?" I asked.

"Ya, mon," said the Innkeeper, going behind the bar and pulling out a bottle.

"Then pass it here," I said. "You hit the wrong head, you drink a shot of tequila."

"Good," said Gus. "I was getting bored with beer and rum."

"Who's throw is it, then?" asked Luis.

"Ernesto's; he's the offended party," I said.

Ernesto pulled the dart out of his shrunken head, and said, "Wonbago," and threw it half way across the room, right into Roger's head, which Gerald was borrowing since he didn't have one of his own yet.

"Damn!" said Wonbago, then he sighed. "Give me di damned rum!" Ernesto's throw had been over six feet, which made it a shot of rum instead of beer.

Everyone had been picking on Wonbago because he was the new guy, and because it was just plain fun since he was so stuffy. He was beginning to get pretty tipsy, and after a few more shots I estimated he'd be ready to go outside and demand to see the hurricane's papers.

"Roger's gonna wonder where all di holes in his head came from," grinned the Innkeeper.

"Give me dat damned dart!" said Wonbago as he wobbled around; he'd started damning everything somewhere around his third shot.

"Get it yourself," said Luis, "It's in your head. Well, Roger's, anyway."

Wonbago went over and managed to grab the coconut on the third try; it wasn't swaying, but he was. He yanked out the dart, and shouted "Damned Jedidididiah!" and shucked it in the general direction of Jed's rather large coconut he'd picked out for himself.

"Ouch!" said Cavin. "Double ouch, dude!"

"Ruling?" said Gus.

"Got any whiskey back there?" I asked.

"Ya," said the Innkeeper, showing me a bottle of Jameson.

"Hit a real person and it's a shot of whiskey," I proclaimed. "Unless of course they're too stupid to get out of the way." Cavin had been standing a good ten feet to the left of Jedidiah's coconut when Gerald's throw stuck him.

"Good, I was getting bored with beer and rum and tequila," said Gus.

"*And* if we think you threw at someone on purpose, it's a shot of Pirate's Poison," I said, guessing Gus' intentions.

"Crap!" said Gus. "Still might be worth it, though."

Pirate's Poison was a special, always changing (so you couldn't build up an immunity to it) concoction the Innkeeper kept in a black bottle with a red skull and crossbones painted on it. It was used to dole out punishment, and whenever it got about halfway down the Innkeeper would fill it with whatever he felt it needed. The one time I saw him top it off it was with Sambuca, scotch, Bailey's, and olive juice. And about half a little bottle of Tabasco.

"Give me dat damned bottle!" said Wonbago. We passed it to him and he tipped it back and took a long pull from it, then set it carefully on the table and fell over backwards onto the floor to sleep.

"One down," said Gus. "Seven to go. Let's move him to one of the benches against the wall."

"I'll help you," said Jedidiah.

"I figured knowing you you'd just want to leave him there," I said.

"Normally I would, but I don't want to keep tripping over him on the way to the bathroom," said Gus.

"I knew there had to be a reason you were almost acting nice," I said. I was finding I liked Gus after all. He was an ornery cuss, but fun to be around, with a good sense of humor. He reminded me of Captain Quint from Jaws.

"Maybe we should take a break," said Cavin.

"Why? It's just getting fun; people are finally starting to pass out," said Gus. "And you're the one who wanted a game."

"Could we find one where we sit at least?" said Luis. "I'm getting tired."

"Fine, old man. We'll sit for a while," said Gus.

I collapsed into a chair as well, grateful for the chance to not stand. The game I'd created had been fun, but too much of anything was too much. And I had the feeling it was about to get ugly with Gus and the steel tipped dart; when Wonbago had stuck Cavin I could tell it gave Gus all sorts of ideas, none of which would be healthy for the rest of us to let him carry out.

Gus sat down across from me again and said "So, Jack; you and Isabella."

"I didn't hear a question in there," I said.

"Is it true? Are you two together?" he said.

I leaned back in my chair as smugly as I was capable of leaning. "It's true."

"Damn! Lucky bastard. First the rum, and now her," said Gus. "I gotta tell ya, when I first met you at the Soggy Dollar there's no way I would've thought you had it in you to get Isabella, let alone to make the rum flow."

"And I would have agreed with you," I said, shaking my head. "I have no idea how the hell either of them happened. But they did, so I guess it was in me after all." The force was strong with this one.

"Let's ask Luis about life; he's the wise old bird," said Gus. "What do you think, old timer? How did Jack pull it off? Luis? Luuuiiis..."

A soft snoring was the only answer we received from him.

"I guess the wise old bird migrated to dream land," I said.

"Two down, six to go," said Gus.

"Six?" I said.

Gus looked around the bar. "Where the hell did everyone go?" he said.

"I think they snuck out under the guise of a bathroom break," I said.

"Cowards!" said Gus, shaking his fist in the direction of the Coconut Motel next door. "Well, I guess it's just you and me, then, alone in a bar; good thing. I was getting bored with beer and rum and tequila and whiskey. Now I can just take my pick from everything." He slid the bottle of Pyrat Rum between us. "So what were we talking about again?"

"Life, and how shit happens," I said. "Although you know what? I'm kind of tired of the question. I've been contemplating my existence for three years now and it's getting boring. Maybe it's time to stop wondering about life and start living it instead."

"I'll drink to that," said Gus, picking up the bottle.

He'd also drank to it being Thursday, and to water being wet, so it was hard to accept his sentiment as being genuine. "Just out of curiosity, though, exactly how did *you* end up here doing what you do now?" I said.

"Well, like I told you back in Van Dyke, I used to work for Delta. They laid me off when the recession hit, so I took a vacation to Anguilla. Three days later I won my plane in a poker game and I've been island hopping ever since."

"And you called *me* a lucky bastard?" I said.

Gus shrugged. "Hey, you made a decision about your life, and my life made a decision about me," he said. "It worked for both of us. But you're the one who got Isabella."

"I am, aren't I?" I said. I started to wonder how that had occurred, then stopped; it was going to be a hard habit to break. I sternly reminded myself that the only thing that mattered was that it did happen, not how. "You know, I love her."

"Great, let's drink to that," said Gus.

"No, I mean, I really love her," I said.

"Who are you trying to convince, you or me?" said Gus. "Or are you just rubbing it in?"

"I'm trying to convince me, although I should know by now," I said. "If it rubs it in to you at the same time that's just an added bonus."

"Well, when you're finished telling yourself and making me depressed there's probably someone else you should let in on it," said Gus.

217

"You're right," I said, standing up. "I do need to go tell someone."

"Right now?" said Gus.

"Now," I said.

"But she's not even on di island!" complained Gus.

"I know that," I said. "I'm going anyway."

"Which leaves me alone in a bar," said Gus. "And it's not even my birthday."

I walked out the back door into the outside area of Monkey Drool's. The wind and rain hit me almost immediately, pushing at me like a firehouse. I pushed back, fighting for yardage towards the beach. It took some effort, especially at my post hurricane party level of coordination, but eventually I got as close to the water as I dared. The ocean was attacking the land with a vengeance, as if it were trying to claw out a beachhead for a full scale invasion of mermaids, and I didn't want to get caught in the crossfire. So I wrapped my arms around a nearby palm tree and held on for dear life.

I had something to tell the world, and the ocean seemed like the best conveyance available to bear my message. I was going to throw my words into its waters and let the tides carry them to all the beaches, where anyone that chose to listen could hear them, including my Isabella. The wind was roaring around my head, but I knew I didn't have to shout; my voice would carry, no matter what. I faced the sea, still tightly hugging the tree as if it were my Latin love, and said "I, Jack Danielson, am in love with Isabella Vaccaria."

I smiled then, content with my little ritual. I carefully let go of the tree and turned my back to the wind, and it pushed me towards the motel, where I needed to go to break the news to my Maria. She'd be heartbroken at first, but hopefully she'd understand that in a way I was in love with her, too, the living embodiment of my hula girl.

I'd gone about twenty wind propelled feet when I heard a loud *"Crack!"* from behind me, followed by an even louder *"Thud!"* next to me that shook the ground as the palm tree I'd been hugging fell to the Earth a few feet away.

I stood staring at the tree as it lay there; again with the almost dying. I tell the ocean I loved my Isabella, and the wind tries to drive me into the ground like a round peg into a square hole. The tree didn't give me any answers, so I looked into the sky for them, the rain stinging my face, my body barely able to keep its balance in the wind. "What does that mean?" I said, pointing at the downed tree. "Am I not supposed to love Isabella? Should I change my life again? What? What am I not getting?"

This was the second time I'd almost been killed in my life, and the third if you wanted to count Rodrigo and *his* Maria. Here I was on a tropical island, all sorts of good friends around me, my first born rum about to come into the world, my beautiful girlfriend, well, out there somewhere anyway, but mine never the less. And now this tree happens? How unlucky could one guy be?

Or much more accurately, how stupid could one guy be?

I turned back to the tree. "I get it now. You're right. You're absolutely right. I hadn't realized it, but it's always been true, hasn't it, even back in Minnesota with the truck and the crashing. Thanks for pointing it out to me, and I promise I won't forget; you can cancel next year's meteorite near miss."

The world was right.

I *was* a lucky guy.

"There's naught no doubt so much the spirit calms as rum and true religion." -Lord Byron

Chapter 24

Twas the night before Rum Day, and all through my hut, not a creature was stirring, except for me. It was close to four in the morning, Rum Eve, and I'd hardly slept a wink.

The first finished rum was about to be born and like any first time father, I was having an anxiety attack.

It was a week after the hurricane party and my watery announcements of love and luck. I hadn't asked Isabella to marry me yet or any such thing, but I was ever so slightly considering it, sometime maybe after the birth of our rum. I know a lot of couples hurry to get married *before* the rum is born, but I wanted to wait; one thing at a time.

My Isabella had nothing to do with why I was nervous at the moment, though; it was all about the rum. One thing that wasn't helping me relax was that I didn't know what to expect from it; Luis had been tight lipped for some time now, when he wasn't shouting at me in Spanish. He'd tried for a while to describe the nuances of what he was doing, but that was uphill work when you're talking to someone like me who'd never paid much attention to taste, other than simply enjoying it.

Hints of vanilla? You either were vanilla or you weren't, unless you were Neapolitan ice cream. Nutty and spicy? Must be buffalo rubbed hazelnuts. Caramel aroma? I understood this one at least, but couldn't recall the last time I'd smelled my rum, except when Cavin had made me laugh and it went up my nose. Obviously I was in need of some serious education, which I was going to get starting with this first batch. But for now I was in the dark as to what exactly was in all those barrels.

The even bigger problem I had though, was that I'd let a terrible thought slip into my mind over the last couple of days; who was this Luis person, anyway? Did he even have a clue about rum, or was he just good at faking it? And if these rums of his he wanted to make for me were so bloody good, then why had he never been allowed to make them before I got suckered into it? It all seemed mighty suspicious now that it was too late to do anything about it.

I'd never really asked Luis about his experience, let alone for any proof of it. I'd basically hired him after the fifteen minute conversation we had near the non grave of my not dead crazy pirate ghost uncle, who had brought him here back in the days he was sailing Mary Jane around the Caribbean. So because my hippie probably stoned at the time relative thought it would be a good idea for Luis to be his factory Master Rum

Blender, I'd decided the same. Perhaps insanity did run in our family, after all.

As the day grew closer I'd slept less and less, growing more and more nervous. What if the rum was bad? Then what? Let Luis cook another batch, wait another year, and hope for the best? I didn't know how I could have been so stupid. Perhaps Luis was perfectly qualified, but that wasn't the point; I should have found out for sure. What if the rum tasted like diet Shasta Cola? That might be fine for a low calorie bargain soda, but it would be a disaster of mythic proportions for us. The lives of everyone on di island rested in the hands of an unknown artist, and it was all thanks to me.

It was obvious I wasn't going to sleep anymore this evening, and perhaps ever again. So I got up and sat on one of the wooden benches around my bonfire circle, a ways down the beach from my hut (floating embers and thatched roofs didn't mix).

It was still dark, an hour or so before the first purple would begin to creep into the eastern edge of the sky. I wouldn't be able to see it from where I was, of course, being on the western side of di island. That was the one disadvantage to where my hut was located, but then again I wasn't usually up early enough to see the sun rise, anyway. I was more of a sunset guy, waiting patiently for the green flash with a fresh papaya and mango daiquiri in my hand, courtesy of the portable

Margaritaville Frozen Concoction maker that Crazy Chester had surprised me with; an appreciation gift for his very groovy birthday bash.

He and Akiko had indeed been seeing each other, but Chester said they were taking things at an island pace. When I asked him what that meant, he said he could maybe see them getting married in about five years if everything went well, which was at island pace, alright. I wondered how Aki would feel about a shirtless groom, but maybe she could talk him into wearing dress trunks, a bow tie, and a cummerbund.; if there was an online Chippendale's store, it might be a good place to start looking for wedding attire.

My Isabella had had a great time in the Keys, although Faith said she was the center of male attention everywhere she went, so I vowed to be with her the next time; until she told me I couldn't come, and then I'd vow to be with her the time after that. I knew in any case I'd want to return, and soon; maybe I'd organize a boys week on my own with some of di island men. There were days I missed my Key West greatly, and all it had to offer to make your life feel like a song.

After annoying the dying embers of last night's bonfire with a stick for a while, I decided if I was going to be up at this hour I might as well see the sun rise, and headed towards the eastern shore. I didn't see anybody during my walk, and it felt like I was the only person on di island; I guess the rest of di islanders had no worries about the rum to keep them awake.

Billy's boat, the Rum Runner, seemed like the perfect place from which to greet Rum Day. The hurricane had pushed her around a bit so her seats hadn't been facing the ocean anymore, but I got a crew together one night at Monkey Drool's and put her back the way she belonged, and replaced her lost pirate flag. I considered repairing her a bit too, maybe a new paint job, perhaps even piece her two halves back together though she'd never be seaworthy again, but it didn't seem right. And something about the way her bow and stern lay there, washed up on the beach apart from one another, was too aesthetically pleasing, even if they told a somber tale. But then most of the best sea stories were sad.

As I sat looking out at the ocean, I could see a blinking light on the horizon, probably a cruise ship making its way to the Virgin Islands. I thought about the thousands of tourists on board, passed out in their racks after a hard day of shopping, eating, and gambling. They'd be oblivious to di island, and there would be more people on that tiny blinking light than on the entire piece of land we inhabited. Of course, up close, their ship wouldn't be so tiny; the first time I saw one, in Key West, I felt like I was standing next to the Imperial

Flagship in dry dock, except the dock was wet, of course.

I didn't think di island would ever be a destination for the behemoths; our port was too shallow, for one thing. But it was difficult to say what the future held for our little home, now that it was slowly growing. A few more people arrived every month now, to try and make a life, and I was still holding out hope for a pizza chef to wash up on shore and open a little corner bistro at the Crossroads. So far though, life hadn't changed much, except for the better, and we weren't exactly overrun with people. But you never knew when some big money real estate developer would arrive and try and buy up land to put up a fancy hotel or condominiums, so poor rich people would have yet another place to get away from it all and be rude to lowly waitstaff.

"Ahoy, matey!" said Captain Black Dog, just as I heard four big paws running up the ramp we'd installed so the first mate could climb aboard on his own. Sammy jumped up and greeted me as always with a big, wet, nose and tongue, then ran around the deck searching for new smells since his last visit.

"Ahoy, Captain," I said, as Billy came on board. He used the ramp as well, which was a lot like boarding an old galleon from the dock.

"Couldn't sleep, lad?" asked Billy, taking his normal seat next to mine.

"What makes you think I didn't just get up early this morning?" I said.

"You? At this hour? Someone would have had to light a keg of gunpowder under your hammock," said Black Dog. "And I didn't hear any explosions."

"Then what about you? Are you always up this early? Or late?" I said.

"Late, laddie. Although bein' a pirate, I'm not much for keepin' time; I sleep when I'm tired and get up when I'm not," said Black Dog. "But I do like the night; it's quiet, and there aren't so many landlubbers about. So what's on your mind this time? You be wearin' one of those faces again, one of those *'I be Cap'n Jack and I'm worried'* looks."

My uncle knew me better than anyone, and that included my Isabella. "I'm just a little anxious about the rum," I said.

"Ah, that's right; it be Rum Day today, ain't it?" said Black Dog. "Well, no need to concern yourself; the rums in good hands. Luis won't let you down; he's got rum in his veins, that one."

"I usually do, too, but that doesn't mean I should be making it," I said. "I know my uncle Billy hired him way back during the original Rum Days, but did you ever hear anything about why he though he was qualified, and why Luis didn't do more in his career?"

It was how I always approached speaking about my uncle with my uncle; talking as if they were two separate people, which in some ways they were.

"Aye, I've heard the tale," said Black Dog. "Your uncle chose him, first, because he felt that deep down, he was a good man. And second, because Luis came from one of the finest rum families in Cuba. You see, back in the day before the changes, Cuba was one of the hottest destinations for wealthy pirates to visit. It had everything; weather, sandy beaches, beautiful senoritas like your Isabella, the finest cigars, and some of the best rums in the Caribbean. And Luis' family had always made some of those rums."

"I've heard part of this, too," I said. "What I'm wondering is why, after leaving Cuba and finishing school, and having that kind of background, didn't he ever-"

"-become a Master Blender?" finished Billy. "One reason; bitterness. It had nothing to do with Luis' abilities, his knowledge. He was so angry about what had happened at home; the evil Spanish Governor Castro stole his family's lands and gave them to the people. And his father protested and died years later in prison. Luis started out with a chip on his shoulder the size of a ship's anchor, and it weighed him down. Even though he manged to keep working in the trade, he never lasted long enough with one company to rise very far. His attitude would get him fired, 'cuz he was always insisting he knew more than his superiors. Yer uncle, though, gave him a chance, and Luis took it; they were both pretty desperate, ya see."

"That explains a lot," I said. "It's hard to believe Luis was ever like that, though; he's so quiet and soft spoken now. Except when he's ticked at me, which seems to be increasingly often these days."

"Don't take it personal, lad. Yer the owner, and Luis has had his battles with them over the years," said Black Dog. "But you're right; he has changed. That's what twenty years of thinkin' will do to ya. Given the time, most people will realize that while some things that happen in this life may be someone else's fault, how you react to them is yours and yours alone."

I felt a lot better, and not just relieved because I knew now the rum was in expert hands. I'd been happy before my little meltdown of doubt to give Luis his chance, but now that I'd heard the whole story, I was even more glad to do so. I'd been lucky in my life that there hadn't been any hardships or tragedies to deal with more difficult than being a Vikings fan every year. It would be easy to look at Luis and his past and tell him to get over it, but not so easy for him to do. And now that perhaps he had finally made peace with it, it was great that it hadn't happened too late like it did for some people.

The sun was beginning to illuminate the sky, and soon it would appear over the horizon. I'd tried once to think of the process as the scientists claimed it occurred, that I was standing on the side of a spinning ball, and it was we who turned our planetary face towards the sun every day, but it was too far fetched for me to buy into. No, the sun was a big, warm, fireball that circled the Earth, just as the moon did, and that was all there was to it. Like Galileo, I would be proven right one day, even if it meant the old Italian lunatic would be proven wrong. Which he was.

"Sammy and I had better find a safe port," said Black Dog, looking at the sky. "Best for us not to be here when the law starts making its rounds; we're still wanted men, ya know."

"Well, come back to your ship later this evening, Captain," I said. "You may find some plunder on board."

"Is that right now? I may do that," said Billy, and he and Sammy disembarked and disappeared up the trail towards his hideout.

I stayed long enough to see the sun rise (note the words; sun rise, not Earth spin). It was my first in a long time, and my first sober in an even longer time, having observed a few at the tail end of some particularly successful beach parties at Monkey Drool's. This one was outstanding, the clouds painted in all the colors of di rum, although I feverishly hoped our rum wasn't going to be pink, too. After the show ended I went to the cantina for breakfast and one of Geeah's spicy omelets, then on to the factory for the start of another new rum song.

"One of the final steps in the rum making process is the mixing together of light and heavy rums of different ages and characteristics by the Master Blender."

Chapter 25

As I went up the stone path that led to the factory, I noticed Jedidiah was standing in the open doorway, his arms crossed. I greeted him with a wave and walked towards the door, expecting him to step aside, but he didn't budge. And if Jed didn't want to move on his own, he wasn't going to move at all.

"Hey, Jed," I said. "Can I get through?"

"No," said Jedidiah.

"No?" I said.

"No," he said. "I be under strict instructions to keep you out."

"From who?" I asked, a bit irritably.

"Luis," said Jed. "He say you been driving everyone crazy all week so you can't come in."

"But it's my factory!" I said. "I'm di boss."

"You be di owner; Luis be di boss," said Jedidiah.

"Yes, but I'm Luis' boss," I said.

"He said if you want di rum to be finished you need to stay away and let him do his job," said Jedidiah. "Or else."

"Or else what?" I demanded.

232

"Or else we be settin' di rum casks on fire," said Jedidiah.

"Now look, Jed, we talked about setting things on fire if you had a problem with me, and agreed it was a no-no, remember?" I said.

"I have no problem with you, boss," said Jedidiah. "But Luis, he do."

"Nice distinction," I said. "Then can you go tell him to come out here so I can at least talk to him?"

"No. Luis say he doesn't want to talk to you, either," said Jedidiah.

"This is mutiny," I said. "Why, if I had a yardarm, and knew what a yardarm was..."

"You can wait on di patio. Luis will bring out di rum around noon, when it's finished," said Jed.

"Are you sure that's okay with Luis? Maybe I should wait out in the water so I'm not touching di island, and someone can swim some out to me," I said.

Jedidiah thought about it. "No, I think di patio should be alright," he said.

Besides not getting any of my cultural references, di islanders weren't very fluent in sarcasm, either, wiping out a full one half of my conversational tools. "Fine; I'll be back later. I'll be damned if I'll sit here and wait outside my own factory like a bad little dog," I said.

"No, you be goin' to do it someplace else," said Jedidiah, with a straight face.

And then there were those times when I thought di islanders might actually be masters of sarcasm instead and I just couldn't tell when they were using it or not.

I had no idea what to do with myself for three hours; although what I really wanted to do now was disappear until mid afternoon and then nonchalantly arrive as if I could care less about the rum. But I knew that wasn't going to happen. The only way I could stay distracted for that long would be a visit with Isabella, and she was refusing to see me too until after the tasting. So I was on my own.

I couldn't understand why everyone was so annoyed with me, especially Luis. I'd simply been asking him a few questions, trying to fully understand the entire process. But he started getting irritated with me when I began querying him about how the different rums were made. I wasn't sure if it was because it was a trade secret or if he felt the owner should keep his nose out of his Master Blender's business. But after tersely answering a few questions he refused to answer any more, and chased me away with a tirade of Spanish.

It was the first time I'd seen him truly angry (although it wasn't going to be the last), and I hadn't meant for it to happen; I'd just wanted to know my business inside and out. But perhaps it was as Billy had said; I was the owner, and Luis had had many bad experiences with bosses, even though many of them had probably been his own fault. And it was possible that like me, he too might be nervous about this first rum. After we got through this beginning and more into a routine, maybe he'd be willing to teach me a few things. But if I was going to learn anything it was going to have to come from him, since Cavin refused to pass on the knowledge that Luis passed to him, citing teacher and student confidentiality.

But if they insisted on keeping me in the dark, I guess it wouldn't matter all that much. I could take on the part of the rum tycoon, signing the checks and strolling through the factory like an ignorant big shot, but staying the hell out of everyone's way. Maybe I'd get a black walking stick and a cream colored suit with a red rose in the lapel. And a panama hat, of course; I had to have the hat. I'd start growing my funny little mustache tomorrow just in case.

I didn't do much of anything for the next few hours. I wandered here and there, taking a time out whenever I found something to keep my mind occupied or emptied. I stopped at the tiny one room schoolhouse just west of the Crossroads and watched the kids play soccer. There weren't many children on di island, just a handful, but that was slowly changing too, as more and more families arrived at the docks.

One of those families, the Clarkes, had come from Barbados where they'd been in the construction business. They were putting up a new farm and hardware supply store at the Crossroads, another sign of progress. Akiko had carried some necessities at the market, but many tools and such had to be special ordered through her. The hardware store meant that other buildings would probably soon follow now that the means to build them would be more readily available.

I sat and watched the work at the construction site for a spell, then gave Marty back stateside a ring. I'd hired him away from Image Makers to be our first sales rep; I wasn't able to pay him as much as his former PR job, but he was more than happy to get away from Mr. Strickland, who had made him his new whipping boy now that I'd vacated the position. Marty had done a great job for us so far; he had a small number of distributors waiting to receive our rum pending a good review from an expert, which Luis had set up in Miami. It seemed that Marty's campaign angle was working, getting us some interest by simply telling our story; the gringo owner who'd inherited the factory from a pirate; our Master Blender, displaced from Cuba, who's family had lost everything to Castro; and di tiny island in the Caribbean from which the rum came.

Marty and I chatted for a while about the rum and how we each were doing. He'd been taking frequent trips to Florida to push our product, which his family enjoyed since it meant time at Disney World and Universal Studios. I'd talked him into visiting di island in the near future; he'd already been to the Keys and out deep sea fishing with Crazy Chester on one of his sales trips, and was going to sail over on the Lizard one of these days. I was very much looking forward to seeing my old friend again.

I still needed to waste some more time, so I went back to the cantina. I wasn't really hungry, but at least I found Roger there, one of the few people at the moment who was still willing to talk to me. We shared an order of Conch Fritters, one my favorites, and Roger told me a big fish story that pleasantly wasted some more of my time. And then I went back to the factory.

It still wasn't quite noon yet, but I couldn't wait any longer, and the patio was always a pleasant place to sit this time of day, shaded as it was by the building. I sometimes forgot how hot it got on di island, having grown used to it by now. But I'd made an effort not to grow used to the beauty around me; the swaying palms, the colorful birds, the white sand beaches, and the incredibly blue sky and turquoise waters. And those were just the obvious things. It seemed I could stop almost anywhere, turn in any direction, and find a photograph staring at me through my eyes. An aged building, a field of wheat or corn, a herd of goats (who still freaked me out a bit); I'd never thought of the tropics as being pastoral, but they truly were.

I let Jedidiah see me as I arrived (he was still dutifully guarding the door), then took a seat at my favorite table on the patio and waited. Before long Luis, Cavin, and Faith came out with a bottle and some glasses on a tray and joined me, evidently taking pity on me since it was only eleven thirty.

I looked at the bottle. "Is this it? Is this the rum? *The* rum? The totally finished, this is what we are going to sell rum?" I asked, wanting to be sure I knew exactly what I'd be sampling.

"It is," said Luis. "This is the final product."

"Hm," I said, examining the clear liquid, somewhat disappointed.

"You don't look very happy, boss," said Faith.

"No, I'm happy, it's just-I thought we might be making something more...interesting. You know, darker," I said.

Luis sighed. "You see, this is one of the reasons I wanted you out of my way. You are too impatient; you want everything to come at once. That's not how you make the rum. Rum is time, years passing, like part of your life. You can't rush living or rum or they will both be bad. And you must wait for some rums longer than others."

"Fine. It's okay, I understand; I was just expecting something else. So what is this exactly?" I asked, indicating the bottle.

"This is where we begin," said Luis. "A simple, but excellent silver rum, good for making cocktails. This is the backbone of our company, something we can make in a year's time. Now we will continue to distill more rums and let them age in their barrels so that I will have many tastes to work with and blend together. In another year we will have two more rums to sell, both, as you say, more interesting. And perhaps we will add even more rums, later. But it will always take time."

"I think I get it, now; it's confusing though, especially to an idiot like me," I said. "So we distill different rums, let them age, then blend them together to make our final product."

"Yes!" said Luis. "Precisely. At last maybe you understand."

"Then today is a great day. We have our first rum, and I don't care what color it isn't. I'm sure it will be good," I said "Let me try it."

Faith picked up the bottle and poured me a glass. "Here ya go, boss," she said, handing it to me.

I took it, and held it up to the light to look at it; I'm not sure why, since it was colorless, but it was what they always did in movies. Then I smelled it, and finally took a sip, swishing it around in my mouth.

"Well?" said Cavin.

"Hm," I said thoughtfully.

"Tell me; what do you taste?" said Luis.

I took another sip; it had very little bite. "I think..." I said.

"Yes?" said Luis.

"I think I taste a bit of vanilla," I said finally.

"Good. And?" said Luis.

I tried another drink. "And maybe...orange?" I said, hesitantly.

"Are you sure?" said Luis. "Be honest. What do you think of it?"

I took one more drink. "Well, no. I'm not sure what I taste. I didn't want to say anything, but to tell you the truth, it's a bit...bland," I said, cringing a bit.

Luis looked crestfallen, and put his head in his hands.

"I'm sorry!" I said. "Maybe it's just me. Or maybe it's better in a drink."

I heard Luis softly chuckling into his hands, and thought he might be losing it.

"Are you okay?" I said. "Maybe my taste buds are screwed up right now; I did have one of Geeah's zesty omelets this morning. And some Conch Fritters. Maybe that's the problem."

"Or maybe," said Cavin. "It tastes bland to you because it's water."

I looked at him. "Water?" I said.

Luis put his head up. "Water," said my three, soon to be unemployed employees, smiling.

"Bastards," I said, and they all started laughing. "Very funny. I'll remember this when I'm writing out your Christmas bonus checks."

"I'll go get the real stuff," said Faith.

The real stuff was mucho tastier than water; I couldn't pick out any particular tastes with my Buffalo Wing trained buds, but Luis said it had the aroma of caramel and toffee, with a subtle, crisp, mango, banana and papaya flavor. I wasn't much for silver rums, but it was good, and I could see how it would be tasty in a cocktail. Which we confirmed later by bringing a case to Monkey Drool's that evening for free rum drinks for di islanders. After some discussion with Luis I decided to call it *"Captain Billy's Swashbuckling Silver,"* to go along with *"Captain Billy's Buccaneer Gold,"* a lightly spiced golden rum due out a year from now. I left a case of the silver on Black Dog's boat; that had been our agreement when he gave me the treasure map that had saved our arses, and this was our finest rum to date.

There'd be more batches of the silver to come, of course, and in another year we'd have other treats to try and be proud of. For now I'd learn to be patient; that seemed easier now that we finally had something to show for all our efforts. I'd stayed on di island to make rum, and at last our first pirate treasure was ours.

Yo, ho, ho.

One Year Later...

"I was like a hermit on a distant mountaintop seeking clarity. A hermit with spiced rum in his hand." -Jack Danielson

Chapter 26

It's November, although I have very few ways to tell, di island not being much for change, even for seasons. Another Rum Day is fast approaching, and though I'm looking forward to it with great anticipation, I keep it in the back of my mind where it belongs. There are things here today that deserve my full attention, and I leave all the worrying about the rum to my Master Blender, Luis, and his able apprentice, Cavin.

The last Rum Day a few weeks ago had been a big success, by my standards. By the time Luis had poured some of his newest elixir into my glass I was almost dizzy with anticipation, although not as dizzy as I would be later that evening after spending it with a full bottle of my very own. But once the Buccaneer Gold had washed over my taste buds I knew every little ting was gonna be alright.

It was delicious; that was my full novice review. A rich amber in color, it would be a great beach or lake rum on a warm summer's day, or any other day for that matter. When Luis asked me what I tasted, continuing my education, I told him chocolate, caramel, pecan, mango, vanilla, nutmeg, orange, coconut, honey, hazelnut and cinnamon. He rolled his eyes and told me we still had a lot of work to do, but I know that sheer odds said I'd had to have been right on at least a couple of counts.

On this next Rum Day to come, our newest product will be available, one I can't wait to try; *"Captain Billy's Black Dog Rum."* I've had Coruba and Cruzan Black Strap, two of my favorites, and Luis said this blend would be somewhere in their fleet; pitch black, with a deep, rich, molasses taste, perfect for drinking while skulking around dark and winding alleys with your disreputable pirate friends. And just over ten short years from now, Luis' masterpiece rum will be ready to make the women (and men) smile like Mona Lisa. It's odd to think that the nine year old's on the planet at the time of its beginnings would be legal to drink it when it finally awakened from its twelve year slumber, but that's life and rum. Good things come to those who wait, though thankfully those of us who are impatient can go out and find them as well, for there are so many good things in life to choose from.

And speaking of good things, I still have every intention of marrying my Isabella one day; just not this day. I'm too damned happy right now; not that getting hitched to a beautiful senorita would make me unhappy, but it would definitely change my life. I still love my shack on the beach, and she's made it perfectly clear that even though I now have plumbing and electricity, she's not about to live there until I tear it down and build something more closely resembling a house. If she ever puts her foot down all the way and tells me it's her or the hut, I suppose I'll marry her, but for now she keeps her knee up in the Captain Morgan position, and I get to have her love *and* my beach bum shack.

Crazy Chester and Akiko are still dating, or else they're not, according to reports coming over the Coconut Telegraph. The truth is, nobody knows for sure what's going on because they keep such a low profile. But Chester is still buying tee shirts from the market he'll never wear, and if that's not true love I don't know what is.

My ex-hippie ghost pirate uncle is doing well, as is his hairy first mate; well enough that it's probably time to drop the ghost part since he seems to be slowly returning to the land of the living. I run into the two of them in more and more new places around di island, and we even saw them sail past during one of my bonfire parties in the new dinghy I purchased for him. I think someday he may even come ashore and join us, but if he never does, I understand.

I just finished my Sunday morning guitar lesson with Cavin a few moments ago. I can almost play along with him while strumming a Buffett tune and not sound horrible now; my next goal is to be able to play solo and say the same thing. The two of us are heading over to

Monkey Drool's; it's heading towards eleven o'clock, and I'm ready for some football on the big screen and satellite dish I finally broke down and purchased for the bar.

The most interesting Innkeeper in the world and I have an agreement; the dish and TV are to be used only for football and movie night Wednesdays, when I pull something out from my DVD collection. The Innkeeper gets more customers, and I get my football and cinema. The rest of the time the television is locked in a waterproof cabinet, for which I and I alone have the key to avoid any sneaky TV watching behind my back. That may sound silly and even mean, but I don't want di island spoiled by the intrusions of the rest of the world; they're bound to come soon enough now that the rum is becoming a modest success.

As Cavin and I arrive at Monkey Drool's I see that Gus, Luis, Jedidiah, Boyd, Jolly Roger, Ernesto and Faith, and Crazy Chester and Aki are already there. So is my Isabella, proving once again that she can look enticing to me even while wearing an Aaron Rodgers Packers jersey. Our household rivalry game isn't this week, but it's coming up soon, so most likely I'll be doing all the laundry and dishes for a week when I lose our twice annual Minnesota-Green Bay bet.

There's nothing that says autumn football like sitting outdoors with your toes in the sand, drinking

Pickled Parrot Punch, and eating Jerk Chicken wings while watching the big game against the backdrop of the blue green waters of the Caribbean. And explaining yet another rule to one of di islanders in their purple Vikings jersey.

I spend my time looking forward and backwards to the now. The past is what brought me here, and the future is the rum to come, and many more days like these. My ship's hold is bursting with the greatest of plunder, so many fond memories that I don't know how or when I'll have the time to look back at them and smile, but perhaps I'll slow my frantic life down one day to enjoy them all.

I suppose maybe I'm still living my life like a Jimmy Buffett song, but I'm not really sure what that means anymore. Things seem pretty parrot friendly to me, but I think the difference is I'm not trying to live like anything anymore. I guess maybe that means I'm happy.

Looks like I'm stuck living my life like a Jack Danielson song.

I hope someday everyone gets the chance to be so lucky.

The End

Made in the USA
Lexington, KY
29 October 2014